The Sprig of Broom

The Sprig of Broom

by

Barbara Willard

decorations by Paul Shardlow

Longman Young Books

LONGMAN GROUP LIMITED
LONDON

Copyright © Barbara Willard 1971

First published 1971

ISBN 0 582 15854 0

Set in 12pt Imprint, 1pt. leaded

Printed in Great Britain
by Ebenezer Baylis and Son Ltd
The Trinity Press, Worcester, and London

Contents

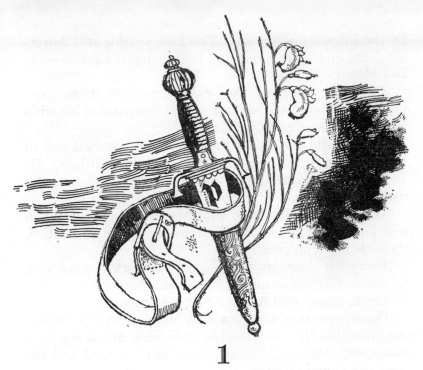

1

Beginning with Richard in 1485

Richard was almost ready for bed when he heard a
clatter on the road and then shouting at the gate. One leg
still in his hose and one leg out, he hopped up on the oak
chest and peered down through the window into the
yard. The window was half horn and half glass—there
were two small panes only, for the room was under the
roof, but the glass pane opened on a pivot. Richard
pushed at it impatiently and squinted down the face of
the house. The hot August night was soft as velvet. The
day had been dry and golden, as though the whole world
took colour from the ripe fields. Now with the rising of
the moon a coolness released the scents pressed in all day

by the intensity of the sun. The honeysuckle still flowering here and there along the hedge might have been in full bloom.

'Open up, if you please!' called the man at the gate; and he reinforced the request with a sharp rap of his whip handle against the iron grille.

Richard did not know the voice. He watched one of the grooms run from the stable, but Matthew, Dr Woodlark's steward, came quickly out of the house and turned him back.

'Wait till I see his face,' said Matthew harshly. 'When will you learn?' Then he slid back the grille and called, 'Who is it? Who's there?'

'From Sir Anthony to Master Woodlark. I pray you, let me in for I have urgent business.'

'Open, then,' said Matthew to the groom.

There were two strangers coming in, but three horses, the third led by the attendant following at his master's command. Men and horses came into the yard and the gate was closed again.

'I am sorry you were kept, sir,' Matthew said. 'My master is particular in these days. We hear nothing but rumours.'

'He is rightly careful. Take me to him, if you please.'

Then they moved out of Richard's view, and only the servant with the led horse remained for him to gaze at in the sharp moonlight. The horse was black and beautiful, so splendidly groomed that even after the ride his flanks shone, his mane and tail flowed as if they had just been combed. The watching boy gulped with nervous excitement. Last time a stranger had come with a led horse it had been to take Richard to a place he had never seen, to be looked over and questioned by a gentleman he did not know—though in the presence of Sir Anthony,

his official guardian. Later, he was returned to Dr Woodlark's, not knowing whether he had passed or failed in
what had seemed to be some test of his person and abilities.
To arrive back at the only home he had known for the
past six years had been at once a relief and a bitter
disappointment. Knowing so little of himself, Richard
had come to expect much. To combat loneliness and
near-despair, he had imagined himself a secret hero, a
prince, a warrior—one to be discovered to his people only
at a precise moment decreed by fate.

If he had been sent for again, perhaps his true situation
was to be revealed at last. His blood ran a little cold.
These were indeed dangerous days. The rumours
Matthew had spoken of were rumours of a great battle
soon to be joined. Then the business would be forever
settled, it was said, between York and Lancaster, between
the reigning White Rose and the rebellious Red. Truly
this had been said often enough about previous battles
on their eve, but truce had never been peace. Now
Lancaster's heir must challenge the Duke of York who
had become King Richard the Third . . .

In a boy's dream of such stirring matters, Richard
imagined how he had been sent for to lead the army into
battle. 'We have waited for such a one as you!' they
would cry—as no doubt they cried to Henry Tudor.
Then there would be banners dipped and swords bared,
and knees bent, and oaths of fealty. He would stand on
the field of victory among his slain enemies, and his own
loyal followers, bleeding but triumphant, would salute
and honour him . . . It was tiresome that since Dr
Woodlark would never speak of politics, it would be
exceedingly difficult for his pupil to tell friend from
enemy. He had no idea on which side he would have
been fighting . . .

4 The Sprig of Broom

He was still at the window, letting his imagination run free and wild, when he heard old Bess's voice calling his name.

'What?' he shouted. 'What is it now?'

He jumped down from the chest and tugged his hose on again. He went to the door and stooped out of it to peer down the narrow stair. The stair was little more than a ladder, the door like the door of a hutch, since in order to have a room to himself, Richard had chosen to make his quarters in the farthest garret.

'Bess?' Richard yelled, for she was deaf. 'What's afoot now?'

'Dress and come to Dr Woodlark,' she said, her face upturned to him. The darkness was filtered by moonlight falling through a small pane in the thatch. Bess was fat and breathless and rested with one hand on her knee, the other clutching the hand-rope. 'Dress now, Master Richard,' she insisted, 'and see thee look spick. Sir Anthony has sent his gentleman for escort. You must ride at once, he says.'

'Ride?' The black horse, shiny and perfect, danced in the eye of Richard's imagination. 'Ride where?'

'The devil himself knows where, God save us all. At such an hour of the night, too. We'll have you growling like a bear this time tomorrow—and sooner.'

'I shan't be here tomorrow, by the sound of it.'

'Get your clothes on, child,' she said, and turned away.

As she went down the stair, Bess moaned to herself, and Richard's heart turned at the sound. That, more than anything else, made him certain that he was moving on. Bess had watched over him for all the six years he had spent in Dr Woodlark's house being educated. It was she who had soothed and steadied him in his misery at being torn from the home he had imagined was his own, where he had been since babyhood, where he had supposed he was born. To be told suddenly, without preparation, without even time for farewells, that he was no kin of the brothers and sisters he had grown up with, that their mother was not his mother, had been so great a shock to a ten-year-old that for almost six months after that he barely spoke, and when he did it was at first with a terrible stammer. Nothing was his own but his name—Richard. It was his only name. No other followed it. For the first time he had discovered that—in law—he had no father.

Richard had greatly needed Bess. Life at Dr Woodlark's was a stern business. No young person ever came to the house and all the servants were old. Dr Woodlark was concerned solely with Richard's education and never spoke to him as to a living person. Rather, he seemed to look upon the boy as a receptacle, a kind of box into which he crammed as much of his own learning as it would contain without the hinges straining and the lid flying off. It was Bess who laid cool cloths to Richard's aching head, slipped him apple pie and sausage when he was punished with bread and water, rubbed his aches when he had been beaten, and cosseted him when he took a fever.

So now when the old woman went moaning down the dim little stairway, Richard knew a spasm almost of nausea. She was bidding him farewell.

He dragged on his doublet, spat on his palms and smoothed down his hair. He went downstairs with so little breath in his lungs that he almost expected to faint as he stood at Dr Woodlark's door.

'Here's the boy now,' the doctor said, tucking in his beard and looking under his eyebrows in a way he had when he was fussed. 'Richard—this gentleman has come some way to fetch you on a journey.'

'Sir—?' said Richard, looking from the old man to the stranger, who was blessedly young. 'Late for journeying,' he mumbled, needing to say something because they both seemed to wait for him. 'Where do we ride?'

'Some miles,' the stranger said. 'I am Christopher Crespin—Kit to my friends. Your guardian Sir Anthony has sent me for you.' He looked rather guardedly at Richard, but with a quirky set to his mouth as if he would smile as soon as ever he felt safe to do so. He was in his early twenties, Richard judged, with a sturdy, rather thickset appearance, not too tall, dressed with style, his fair hair cropped unusually short but still long enough to curl a little behind his ears. 'You stand very straight, Master Richard,' he said.

'Should I not?' asked Richard, puzzled.

'You should—you should. But some stand crooked— that is all.'

'You had best be on your way,' Dr Woodlark said, and he sounded impatient. 'They have brought you a mount, boy—which is as well, for God knoweth my stable cannot offer much.'

'Let's ride, then,' Crespin said, moving at once.

'When shall I return, sir? What shall I take?'

'A warm cloak. It is a hot night but all dawns are chilly.'

It was a half answer. Richard looked for help to Dr Woodlark but there was little hope in that direction. The doctor wore the air of one finishing off a bit of business and glad enough to turn to some new task. His manner was a dismissal. Richard knew then certainly that when he left this house he would not return.

The black horse was so sweet a mount he might have

been bred solely to carry young Richard. Richard's way
of life had been restricted and he had had little chance of
becoming more than a merely competent rider. The horse
seemed to accept this without rancour. His action was as
smooth as his coat, his mouth tenderly responsive.

'He needs neither curb nor spur,' Master Crespin said.
'Love him and he will love you.'

'Has he a name?'

'What horse has not? You must call him Sceptre.'

'And he might carry a king as a king carries a sceptre!'
cried Richard, glad of the opportunity to show at least
a little wit, and encouraged to find he had spirit enough
in him, at this low hour, to choose the words.

'He might—he might, indeed,' replied Crespin. 'It is
a right royal name, and he is proud and noble, masterful
yet gentle. Isn't that what royal means—and how kings
and horses alike should always be?'

There was not quite light enough, even from this great
moon, for Richard to see his escort's expression. But he
took the words to be a little ironic, and the tone of voice
to suggest that few horses and few kings came up to such
high expectations.

They were now turning out on to a wider road and
Christopher Crespin gathered up his reins.

'We have a stiffish ride,' he said, 'so be ready to put
your back into it. Sceptre shall do the rest.'

'Where are we bound?'

'I am poor at explanations.'

'What is to explain, sir? I only need a place name.'

'Then say it is not in my brief to supply your need.
I will tell you one thing, however, in case you feel sorely
treated. Where you are going you will be welcome, though
your stay may not be long ... We must be on our way
and no more chattering. Settle in your saddle and let

Sceptre have his head. He'll see you come to no
harm.'

With that Crespin put his horse into a canter and
Richard—or Sceptre—quickly followed. The servant
brought up the rear. He, too, was well mounted, which
seemed to suggest he was in good service; the nags ridden
by Dr Woodlark's servants were as gnats to butterflies
in this connection.

The clear night streamed over Richard's shoulders
like a mantle. The shadows laid by the moon seemed red
and purple under the silver sky. This was a flattish
countryside, almost the middle of England, and they
were riding west by north. Sometimes they passed other
riders, sometimes knots of men walking, others trundling
carts. All were moving in the same direction. It could
not, surely, be chance that led so many to be on the same
road. So much traffic by night, even in summer moonlight, was unusual. True, it was the harvest moon that
lit them on their way, and men worked at such time to
midnight and beyond. But these were not harvesters—
at least they would not harvest grain. It came to Richard
then that they were all, himself included, moving towards
that great battle between York and Lancaster that had
long been predicted. He knew of this only through the
servants, since Dr Woodlark would never discuss such
matters. He knew that the Lancastrian claimant to the
throne was Henry Tudor, Earl of Richmond, who had
long been in exile in France. If there was to be a battle,
then he had landed and gathered his supporters into an
army. Within a matter of hours, perhaps, the crown of
England would be both lost and won.

'We are not the only travellers,' Richard said, when
Kit Crespin reined in after a good stretch and walked his
horse.

'The nearer we get, the more there'll be besides us. Men smell out a fight as crows smell carrion.'

'And shall there be a fight?'

'Yes.'

'A battle?'

'A battle royal. King Richard has raised his standard. The Earl of Richmond is marching against him. His claim to the throne of England is a strong one. Thousands will follow him.'

'Are you taking me to fight?' the boy asked, his blood pumping in his ears in terror and excitement.

'Not you. No.'

'Then—?'

'I have already said my orders are not concerned with giving you information. You must be patient.' Crespin gave a slightly uneasy shrug. 'Talk of other things.'

'It was the same last time,' Richard complained. 'Sir Anthony sent for me, and I was taken where I had never been before.'

'But you know Sir Anthony well.'

'He comes every quarter to Dr Woodlark's. He pays my keep and gives me money for my purse. And before— before I was there—I did—I did s-sometimes s-see him.' He stuttered over this bit because he still did not care to remember being ten years old and torn without warning from everything he knew. 'I know him by name and face, that's all.'

'Oh, aye,' agreed Crespin. 'And there's many one knows no better, nor ever will, though they're met with every day. But go on with the story while we rest the horses. You were sent for—taken to a strange place . . . ?'

'It was a castle, sir. There was a tall gentleman in a fine doublet who questioned me.'

'About?'

'My life. My lessons. Set me problems I must answer at once. Asked how strong I was. What weight I could carry and had I ever worn armour, and how was I a-horseback.' Richard wriggled a little, for he found the memory humiliating. 'Made me show my muscles. Called in a lad twice my size and had us wrestle.'

'Did you do well?'

'No. I was thrown on my shoulder. I tell you—he was twice my size.'

'What then?'

'Sir Anthony led me from the castle and his servant rode me home. I liked that, for he's a good sort of fellow—very fiery. He said there should be a battle soon. And this is it—the battle ahead of us now? That's true, is it not, Master Crespin?'

'True as light, true as heaven and hell! And you shall call me Kit, if you please, Richard—for we may find we have much in common. I would answer all your queries, if I could. But answers have a way of staying hid.'

'That's nothing new,' Richard said in a bitter voice. 'Since I discovered I am not the boy I seemed, *No* and *Nothing* and *Not now* are the replies I know best. I am Richard Nothing. I am surely a bastard and have no rights ever of kin or property.'

'Well,' said Kit Crespin laughing, 'you are not the only man in the world who cannot claim his father. But do not call yourself names—leave that to those who dare. I always tell the world I was born an orphan!'

At this moment the servant called out, 'Sir! There is a great flurry on the road behind us. We had best draw aside.'

Crespin wheeled his horse instantly, and Richard's fine Sceptre followed into the shadow of the trees lining the road. The servant's cry had broken in on Crespin's laugh, and there was at once a feeling in the air of heightened awareness, of anticipation, excitement, even fear. The 'flurry' resolved itself into the thud of hooves and a party of twenty or more swept by at a stretched gallop. A cloud of dust rose about them and by the time it cleared they were already out of sight.

'They are riding to the battle,' Richard said. His voice wavered, and again there was the thump of his own heart like a muffled hammer inside his ear. They will fight, he thought; they will die. It was an heroic statement. But then he thought: First they may be wounded. Cold steel will pierce them and hack them. They will lose arms and legs, they will be gashed mortally and the hot thick blood will fill their eyes and their lungs. Then only they will die, in pain and desolation, and all to decide which man of two shall wear a crown.

In the east, almost behind them, the first hint of daylight might have been only the reflection of the fast setting moon, yet it was enough to show that by now there were great numbers on the road. As Crespin led them again to a gallop they came all the time on more and more people. There were not only those who rode or tramped, but others who were now resting along the verges. Some had great packs into which they had stuffed such belongings as they might need. There were many cooking pots slung over eager fires, and now there rose in this faint dawn an appetising smell that made Richard's mouth water. Some of those who journeyed had with them their entire families—wives, children, small babies.

'But *they* cannot fight!' Richard shouted to Kit Crespin.

'They go as ravens go—for the pickings!' Crespin reined in and the pace of all three slowed. 'The more the dead, the more the chance of gain. Some corpses have

2

gold about them, as anyone knows. Others fine jewels, rings and pins for the taking. And there are always cloaks and boots and hose and leather jerkins. Suits of mail, my boy, to be sold to the highest bidder. Any field of battle, come nightfall, will have its rats and crows.'

'Is it truly so?'

'Why not? What does a dead man need more than a shroud, be he knight or soldier . . . But come on, now, Richard Nothing. It must be all of four o'clock. I swore to be there sooner. Remember I did promise you one certain thing—that where you are going you will be welcome—'

'—though my stay may not be long . . . But that's just one more mystery.'

'Make haste to solve it, then,' said Kit Crespin.

Now they rode steady and hard, their purpose all in their arrival. As they went the road became increasingly busy. Sometimes they passed orderly marches of a hundred and more, their leader mounted and attended by a standard bearer. The arms of many gentlemen might thus be seen, though still dimly in the pale dawn. Those who marched behind such men followed them in the old feudal way, turning their backs on country pursuits, leaving the last of the harvest to their wives and old fathers, to whom they might never return.

The sombre dim morning, warm with summer, was yet chill with farewells and pain. Following after Kit Crespin, Richard tried to swallow his dread that he, too, might be expected to share in this man's-work; he, too, might die. Because Dr Woodlark had been so chary of politics Richard was not even sure where his loyalty should lie. Was he York or Lancaster, for the King or for the Earl?

The horses were now very blown and again Crespin dropped to a walk.

'Where is the King now, then?' Richard asked, warily, groping his way round the problem.

'Hard by Leicester.'

'Then all these about us are for York—for King Richard?'

'If not—they are sent as spies. The Lancastrians will be mustering out of the west,' Crespin said.

Richard's problem was solved—but he was not so sure he would not rather be riding to take up arms for the rebel.

'Then the King must surely win the day,' said Richard.

'There are other roads than this, with other travellers— and there could be more of them,' Crespin replied.

At this moment the sky cleared to let through the rising sun. Ahead, without warning, there rose up a great concourse of men converging on a billowing city. Mist wreathed over the field but already a breath of wind shifted and thinned it, so that these castles of silk and linen bellied a little, banners and pennants flapped lazily. The frail battlements, no more than decoration to a hundred pavilions, bowed slightly in the morning breeze. The bones of the tents showed clear as the skeletons of leaves when a wet wind turns them. As the increasing sunlight whisked off the last of the mist, the colours and devices on the standards and the big flags blazed into colour, and their devices shone clear—checkey and chevron, beast and bird and tree, argent and azure and blood on gold.

Even at a distance there was a great noise over the field. The blacksmiths were at work, shoeing and riveting, working on man and horse alike.

Kit Crespin touched up his own mount, and the three of them cantered on. On the edge of the city of tents they were challenged but let through on Crespin's word. Then he halted and at last Richard was offered the beginning of an explanation.

'There is a gentleman here who has sent for you all this way. There will not be much time to greet him. Make the best of it—you may never see him again.'

'What gentleman?' Yet he knew even as he asked the question. 'My father,' he said, stating, not querying.

Before Crespin could reply, Sir Anthony came thrusting through the press towards them, looking stern and angry, calling loudly to Crespin, 'You've taken time enough to get here!'

'It's a fair step, sir. We came as well as we could—I have brought your ward, as you see.'

Sir Anthony looked up at Richard, still in the saddle, and the boy could not read his expression now any more than on earlier occasions. Yet a certain change in Sir Anthony's voice as he spoke to him caused Richard some uneasiness. He did not want to learn that this cold gentleman was his father.

'Are you well, Master Richard? Have you been told why you are here?'

'Only that—'

'I said, Sir Anthony, this second past and no sooner, that his father had sent for him.'

'Dismount and follow me,' Sir Anthony ordered. He snapped at Crespin: 'Speak lower.'

Richard slid from the saddle and almost fell on the ground. He was so stiff he could have groaned aloud, only there were more urgent matters to attend to. He was buzzing with the shock of Crespin's almost casually spoken words—of their confirmation by Sir Anthony.

Your father, Crespin had said. And: *Make the best of it—
you may never see him again . . .*

To see him once seemed to Richard almost too much to
face. He stumbled after Sir Anthony, trying to straighten
his back, tugging down his doublet, pushing his hair
under his cap.

A soldier, a pikeman, on duty at a tent flap, saluted and
stepped back.

'Straighten your shoulders, boy,' Sir Anthony said.
'Take off your cap. Master Crespin has told you who you
are to see.'

'My father, sir.'

For an instant Sir Anthony seemed to hesitate. His face
softened and he put his hand on Richard's shoulder.

'There now,' he said quite gently, 'life is not always
fair or easy, Richard. Come, boy—there's not much time
to lose. We shall be fighting soon.'

He pushed Richard ahead of him into the little ante-
room of the tent, where a page was polishing at a big
helmet, rubbing it with his sleeve. A guard held the flap
aside and then they were in the big tent itself.

Maps and plans were spread on a trestle table, with a
number of gentlemen, half armed, gathered round and
discussing this or that.

'This is the boy, sir,' Richard heard his guardian say.

One of the gentlemen turned instantly and even eagerly.
Richard saw, most strangely, his own face, changed by
time and trouble, yet instantly recognised. He shook and
trembled with shock. His mouth stretched to a smile, but
his eyes filled with tears. They stood for a second staring
at one another, the sturdy dark man, the uncertain boy.
All the others in the tent fell gradually silent.

'I'll talk to him alone,' the dark man said.

2
Proceeding with Medley in 1506

The old priest sometimes dozed off during lessons towards
the end of the day. Medley and Roger, Giles and Hal, who
were his only pupils, took advantage of the old man's
gentle snores to play dibs or marbles until a sudden loud
snort gave warning that their master was about to open
his eyes. He always did so very warily, not admitting even
to himself that he had slept.

'Now stand to construe the next passage, Roger
Mallory,' he would murmur; though they might have been
deep in calculation when slumber took him.

Of the four boys, only Medley Plashet was a poor man's
son. Roger Mallory's father kept the manor of Mantle-

mass; Giles Ade was the miller's son—his grandfather had been a great miser and thus improved the family fortunes; Hal might do better than any of them, for he was the son of Master Urry whose big iron furnace and forge had been begun a generation earlier—the iron trade was increasing all the time nowadays. Medley, however, was unlikely to inherit any more than his father's brain and his mother's kind diligence; but perhaps that was not such a bad fortune.

'Medley, meddler, son of a pedlar!' Hal Urry liked to chant. Medley suffered a good deal because of his name; even Sir James, the old priest, declared it to be ungodly.

Although Dick Plashet, Medley's father, had half a dozen skills without abiding by one trade, he certainly was no pedlar of his labour. Indeed it might have been better for Medley and for his mother if Plashet had not been too proud to seek out employment. He waited for it to come to him—the favour must be on his side. This could lead to hard times, though mostly he was in reasonable demand, for he was a useful man. Before he came to settle in these parts he had served a London apprenticeship to a master builder. He was skilled as both carpenter and joiner. Besides, he could read and write not only English but Latin; he possessed books of his own which he kept wrapped in cloth and tied into a leather bag, near enough to the hearth to keep them free of damp. And in the years that he had been about the forest he had made himself so conversant in all its tracks and secret ways that he was much in demand as a guide.

Sir James taught his pupils as much about the forest as about more conventional matters—how once the southern weald, or *wild* as they still called it hereabouts, had been dense forest over all this edge of England, with many wild animals abounding, so that it became the hunting ground of kings.

'And even in the days of King Edward, third of the name,' he would tell them, always in the same words, so that they mouthed it with him and almost stifled themselves with silent laughter, 'there were no less than seventeen guides in succession needed to conduct him north to south.'

That was well over a hundred years ago, but Sir James was so steeped in the mysterious past that it seemed to him quite recent—indeed it would have been in the lifetime of his own father, for Sir James was now over eighty years old. For sixty of those years he had been chantry priest up at the old ruined palace on the forest, where the chapel had remained consecrated and in use until its roof, like the palace's, fell in. Now he lived in a two-room dwelling at the church porch in Staglye village, and it was there he held his school. He had almost outlived this home, too, for it was in a sadly ruinous condition, and must surely be rebuilt before much longer.

Sir James's pupils found his obsession with the countryside most useful, and would lead him on diligently, as far as ever possible from whatever subject might be causing them difficulty.

'And did you ever see a royal hunt in the forest, sir?'

'Which King Edward was it built the palace?'

'Have you poached a stag, ever in your life?'

'Please, father, tell us about the wars . . .'

'Were you for York, Sir James, or for Lancaster?'

This would be sure to sting the old man into sharp retort that the forest had long been named for that Duke of Lancaster who had it by barter from the King his father—and if it was named so, then for certain most men living about the place were Lancastrian followers. So by force of circumstance alone they were usefully on the winning side.

'But it's all long over,' he would end. 'Praise God, no man need fight his brother now . . . England is quiet. The King sits firm. We are blessed in King Henry—'

'Seventh of the name,' mouthed his pupils, hugging their ribs and spluttering into their palms.

Sir James always spoke as though England had been totally untroubled in these last twenty years since the death of the Yorkist King Richard III on Bosworth Field. Medley was better informed. His father always knew about such things. Perhaps it was because he had lived in London when he was a younger man that he remained sharply interested in how the world went. No doubt he gathered information, too, from the travellers he guided through the forest, setting them on the road for the coast or on towards Kent. Medley often thought with pride that many a traveller must have been astonished to find a peasant able to converse so well, and with so much intelligent curiosity. He did not speak like a peasant, either, unless he had some purpose in roughening his voice and using words that Medley and his mother used by instinct. There was no one in the neighbourhood who knew so much about the affairs of the time as Dick Plashet—about the King and the court and the doings of Parliament, and matters of warfare and statecraft—not even the people at the manor, for all their high connections, knew as much. So it was Medley who was able to tell his schoolfellows that the country had been a good deal less quiet than Sir James would let them believe. There had been war with France for one thing, and royal marriages, and rebellions against the new monarchy, the House of Tudor, that had combined the Yorkist and Lancastrian factions after Bosworth. It had never been proved, Medley boasted, that young King Edward V and his brother had died in the Tower, and because of it there had been a whole handful of pretenders claiming to be one or other of the young princes grown to manhood in hiding.

'My father says it would be none of their own fault,' Medley told the others. 'There'd be masterful villains ordering them, he says.'

'My father,' said Hal, 'do say your father's too clever by half.'

'Beat him for that, Melly!' the other two always roared at such an exchange. 'Colour his eye! Down him, Melly!'

'He'm too small and timmersome,' Medley would reply with dignity. Which was true, though cruel; poor Hal was dreadfully undersized. It was said his father put all his muscle into forge and foundry and spared none for his children, who were without exception weedy.

Between a school of four there was not much need for factions, and they did not quarrel much. Or they vented their spleen and had done with it in a battle of York and Lancaster. Medley never minded being York because he always felt his father had a sneaking allegiance to the defeated. He had never said so, but he had spoken up for the pretenders. When he told the tale of poor Lambert Simnel, humiliated to the status of kitchen boy, he told it with a kind of sad tenderness. For young Warbeck he had expressed less approval, but said he never should have been condemned to death. There were others, too, that Medley could not remember by name. One it was easy to remember had been an Earl of Warwick, and another Earl of Suffolk—he was still alive. In fact during this very summer Medley's father had picked up a tale of the young man's capture, and how he had been paraded through the streets of London before being thrust out of

the fine June weather into the dripping darkness of the
Tower. This made Medley shudder more than all the tales
of vile execution. . . .

It was summer still as the four boys sat and listened to
Sir James's gentle snores in the hot little schoolroom. A
crowd of flies buzzed and bumped under the rafters,
sometimes descending to the old man's forehead, where
they crawled over the furrows in his brow until they woke
him. Outside the light was yellow and the fields ripening.
As he woke, Sir James was saying—just as if he had never
closed his eyes—

'And so it is my wish, and that, I trust, of your good
parents, that the school shall close this fortnight coming.
We shall all have a time of holiday. For truly, if you do
not need it, your old master does.'

They leapt up and cheered, hurled their slates about,
dug one another in the ribs, grinned widely and foolishly
at the thought of delights ahead.

'When does it start, father?' Roger was asking Sir
James. 'Is it now?'

'It is now,' the old man agreed. He smiled under his
eyebrows at his pupils. 'God knoweth you are not such
bad boys,' he said. 'I have taught more boys than you,
and not all were so much better, after all. Be off, you
ruffians, and leave me to my prayers.'

They just remembered to go and kneel for his blessing
before they bounded out of the stuffy schoolroom and
into the shimmering light of late afternoon. They ran
across the churchyard for the sport of leap-frogging over
the most convenient tombstones, then shouted as they
hurled themselves on the grass and rolled down the
mound on which the church was perched. They pelted
across the village street and scrambled to the top of the
further mound, which was called the castle, then rolled

down that. Cows grazed in the field. Roger got dung on
his good green jerkin. Hal, bellowing, rolled into the
bramble patch halfway down the slope and came out
scratched and torn about the face and hands. Medley
cracked his knee on a boulder and made a rent in his only
good hose, but Giles just avoided the vicious bed of nettles
that was the worst hazard. None cared. When they parted
and took their different ways home, they were still running.

Medley and Roger Mallory set out together. The forest
thickened as they slowed on the first steep track. Then
suddenly the urgency to get home drained out of them
and they began to loll and loiter, to discuss matters that
were between the two of them and excluded Hal and
Giles. They shared the same quarter of the forest, while
Hal went off sharply westward and Giles cut away on
the longest journey of all to the mill; that meant they also
shared everyday matters, fishing and hunting, important
talk about the future, grumbles about their parents, and
occasional worries about sins committed and punishments
looming.

'We'll fish the pool tomorrow,' Roger said.

'Yes,' agreed Medley, and made no other comment,
though this was something of a milestone. Until now
Roger had fished with him anywhere else, but not at the
pool which, he had hotly declared, was part of his mother's
property. It could not be, for the pool was deep on the
forest, and Medley had been unable to let the statement go.

This was perhaps their only quarrel and to find it
suddenly set aside was enough to cause Medley's heart
to swell with pleasure. His obstinacy urged him to remark
on a change of heart, but he had lately found himself
able to hold back and keep silent at such moments. His

admiration for Roger, his gratitude for his friendship—
Roger was two years older, besides being in a far better
situation in life—caused him to smile without any
triumph.

'I made a rare boffle of my hose,' he said, to change
the subject. He picked at the rent and pulled a long face.
'I'll get a middling dish o' tongues from my poor
mother.'

'My brown hose are too small and not much worn,'
Roger said. 'Have 'em and welcome. Wait when we come
to Mantlemass and I'll fetch them to you.'

Mantlemass, Roger's home, sturdily built and about
fifty years old, stood on high ground. It commanded a
wide sweep of forest, and the farm buildings were close
at hand, huddling about it as a town might huddle about
a castle for care and protection. Lately many newcomers
had settled at Mantlemass, building themselves roughish
dwellings of stone and timber with thatched roofs. Forest
had been cut back to give the new dwellings room, and
to supply timber for more barns and sties, as the stock
increased with the increase of labour to care for it. The
fine beechwood that stood like a rampart behind the house
had been thinned because of all this. While Roger's
great-aunt was alive it had not been possible to touch
the beeches because of her strong views about conserving
timber. She had died three years ago, and after a decent
interval the work had been put in hand. Roger's mother
had said that one day Mantlemass would be a village,
and that to bring this about they must build a church,
for the increasing numbers of people attached to the
manor and the farm already filled to overflowing the little
chapel belonging to the house.

Today, the whole of Mantlemass was bustling with
preparations for harvest. No one had time for more than

a glance at the two boys. There had been an outstanding hay crop off the upland meadows belonging to the manor, and Roger's older brother, Simon, was helping to thatch the biggest rick. He paused just long enough to shout that since Roger was home he had better set to work. 'And set that Medley Plashet to work, too!' he bellowed, grinning hideously at Medley, but in the friendliest possible way. Because his mother had been the manor reeve's second daughter, Anis Bostel, Medley was entirely accepted at Mantlemass; and though when they were both older he might find he must touch his cap to Simon Mallory, that time was not yet.

They were thatching with reeds, Simon and two other men, and a smaller boy was lugging up bundles of the reeds from the quantities suspended along the barn wall to dry.

Roger cried out at the sight of the lad. 'My old brown hose! You're wearing my hose! Come here! I need them!'

The boy dropped the reeds and clasped himself hard about the waist. He ran, and Roger ran after him, with Medley on his heels. The hose were sheared off above the knee, so they were not much more use than Medley's own, which was a sad disappointment.

The three went pelting across the rickyard. Roger caught up with the smallest as he began to scramble over the low stone wall.

'I'll have them off you!' Medley heard him shout. He dragged at the boy and lifted him up bodily. A thin scream accompanied such a violent threshing of arms and legs that Roger was knocked backwards. 'Catch her!' he yelled to Medley. 'It's Puss in my clothes, you fool! Catch her and deal her the bannicking she deserves!'

Medley burst out laughing. He ran at Puss Mallory with his arms in the air, making a monster's face, lolling out his tongue and squinting. They went round and round the smaller of the ricks and he finally tricked her by doubling back.

'Treat me like a lady!' she instantly demanded, flat on her face with Medley leering above her. 'You gurt ugly lout—keep your hands off me!'

'Puss, Puss, pretty Puss!' mocked Medley, his foot hovering over the small of her back and pushing her flat every time she heaved herself up. But he was weak with laughter and she seized her chance. She rolled away and leapt to her feet, springing at him so violently that he fell flat in his turn. Puss knelt on his chest, tugging at his hair and making talons over his eyes in threat of what she would do to him. 'Pax!' moaned Medley.

Simon's voice came ringing over the yard. 'Catherine! Kitten! Puss! Bring some more reeds! If you must look like a lad, then work like one!'

Catherine rose at once, spurned the prostrate Medley sharply, first with one foot then with the other, and stalked back to her task.

'Satan's brat!' Roger yelled after his sister. 'I'm sorry, Melly. I'll bring you a decent pair of hose tomorrow to make up for her, I swear it.'

'Let her be,' Medley grinned. 'Maids get little sport, seems me. Two year on, she could be wed and bound for life. Poor Puss.'

'When you're my age,' said Roger, quite kindly, 'you'll know that women have their place and should keep it.'

'Like I hear your good mother's aunt did keep it,' Medley said slyly. 'Argue and beat any man, she could, so my mother tell me.'

'Get off home, you!' said Roger, bunching up his fists, but grinning just the same.

Medley parted from Roger and went on past the last

outpost of Mantlemass, over the river and up the far
bank, through the wood and even beyond. On one
horizon, very briefly, he saw the black gaping ruins of
the old palace which no one now could remember seeing
whole. Then he plunged briefly into fifty acres or so of
woodland, with a charcoal-burning in a clearing at its
entry. At last he emerged from the cool dark into the
brazen evening of a day that had been hot as a furnace,
and saw his home ahead of him, facing down a little
ghyll, smoke rising from the roof, and his father outside
the door talking to a stranger.

3
From London

His father looked across the water and saw the boy on his way. He smiled and raised his hand and Medley waved back as keenly as if they had not met for days. His father was a strangely withdrawn man, and when he smiled Medley felt his own spirits bound up. The stranger turned to look where Dick Plashet was looking. Medley ran down the slope, jumped the water and pounded up the bank to the cottage. As he came near he heard the stranger say, 'Even liker his father than you were.'

And Medley's father answered, 'I am sorry for it.' Which struck Medley as overly modest, for his father was surely a rather handsome man. The boy hesitated as he came near, wondering if he should wait till the stranger had gone. But his father called out to him, 'Come here and pay your respects to Master Crespin. He has ridden a long way to see me. And after long years.'

'Sir,' said Medley, and made a decent bow. He did not pull his forelock as a country lad might, and the country sound left his voice.

'What's your name?' Master Crespin asked.

'Medley, sir. Medley Plashet.'

Master Crespin raised his eyebrows and cried, 'Well, Medley's a name I never heard till now.'

'And that's one reason it was chosen,' Dick Plashet said. 'A name that neither you nor any other could know, now or tomorrow or the day after. For that matter his fortunes are a medley. And when he was born they laid him on a cloak of tawny-medley that was across his mother's bed. Now, Kit Crespin, you are answered.'

'Then—Plashet,' said the visitor, sounding a little sly and near to laughter. 'I have not always called you Plashet, Richard.'

'Names get re-spun in a country fashion. Plashet is a name these people know.'

Medley looked from one to the other of the two men. He was bewildered and felt almost as if he was being mocked by both of them. Truly his father was not one who made easy confidences, yet surely he should have spoken of a man he seemed to know as well as he knew this Master Crespin. The look on his father's face, however, was one he knew well, a stubborn, closed look, a refusal to take part in what was immediate. Master Crespin seemed to know the look, too, for he shrugged and grimaced.

The visitor was a very pleasant-looking man coming up to middle-age—forty or so, Medley supposed, since he judged him older than his father, and he was in his late thirties on his own admission. Master Crespin had thick grey hair but you could see that it had turned grey from fair, and there was still a slightly yellow sheen here and there. Medley's father was dark with white streaks. Both men were of medium height and thickly built. But for their colouring they might from behind have been taken for brothers. For that matter, they were not unlike in the face, though there were many differences. They seemed the same sort of man, but made individual by their differing circumstances. Master Crespin's clothes were rich, and the horse tethered at the well-head was a fine creature. Dick Plashet's horse came of good stock, but got a sparse living at times, and its bones showed. The contrast between the two men and their two animals was almost painful. As he looked from one to the other Medley felt his face burn, and he moved instinctively to his father's side, standing close and looking defiant.

Dick Plashet lifted his hand as though he would put his arm across the boy's shoulders, but then he changed his mind and let his hand drop. It would have been unusual for him to offer the embrace. His reserve was enormous. He rarely even took his wife by the hand. He kept his affections like a hawk on its perch. Perhaps twice Medley had seen the bird unhooded—once when his sister died in her second year; once when his mother was struck by a falling bough when she was out herb-gathering and was carried home as dead. Then indeed Dick Plashet had been moved out of his careful calm, and his despairing calling of her name had made the neighbours who were helping turn away . . .

Anis came out of the house now, conveniently breaking the curious stillness that had touched the three by the well.

'Bring your guest indoors, Goodman Plashet,' she said.

She was little and sturdy, round-faced and brown, with an apple-flush accentuated by her white head-kerchief. She looked what she was, the country daughter of country serving folk, and the country was in her voice and her manner of speech. She was strong and full of humour, yet there could appear in her a wariness, a cool dignity hard to understand.

'Here is an old friend, mistress,' Dick Plashet said. 'This is Master Crespin—Kit Crespin. I think I have spoken of him.'

'Aye, so you have,' she agreed, surprising Medley. She made a quick courtesy and looked the stranger in the eye with careful courage. And Master Crespin returned the look, bowing, and smiling gently. 'Well, sir,' she said to him, 'come you in, then. Not much to offer, but what there is—that's yourn as good as ourn.'

'God bless you, dame,' said Crespin.

'Medley,' she ordered, 'run you and set out ale and the good wine. There's a pie out of the oven. Off with you.'

Medley ran. His mind was bursting. So little had been said, so much conveyed—yet mysteriously so. His father talking in riddles, the stranger seeming to know everything yet nothing; then his mother's bracing of her shoulders as she faced him . . . Medley rushed indoors and pulled the wine cups from the cupboard. His father had made them out of apple wood, so perfectly proportioned, so smooth that they were as good for their purpose as if they had been gold or silver. He set them on the table, and then flung down to the cellar and pulled a jug of ale and a smaller one of wine. He carried them carefully upstairs, dropping the trap behind him with his toe. He heard the voices of the others as they approached the house. His mother was talking hard. She would never be told harshly to hold her tongue, as many women were. Medley put down the jugs without slopping, then looked about for the pie. As he rushed it to the scrubbed table it began to slide on its platter. He just managed to save it and get it into its place with the jugs and the cups as his mother came through the door. Master Crespin stood back and bowed her in as if she were a lady; and she took the courtesy worthily.

They sat at table and Medley poured wine for Master Crespin.

'It is all of fifteen years since your father and I drank together, Medley. And that, as I recall, was in a London tavern by the river. A great deal has happened since then.'

'And do you come this way from London, sir?' asked Medley—remembering not to call it *Lunnon*, but only just in time. 'I'll go there one day, I reckon.'

'Send for me and I'll be your guide. That's a promise.'

'Did you ever see the King?' asked Medley, pausing with the jug in the air above his father's cup.

'Yes, for sure. This King and the last one, too. They say His Grace is an ailing man. Two of his sons have died already, so we must pray Prince Henry lives to take the throne.'

'And if he should not—?'

'Stop chattering and sit down,' his father said.

'Ah, Medley, there's always a claimant for any throne, whether it's occupied and whether not. Men enjoy strife and danger.'

'Oh yes, sir—I know about that. Like Simnel and Warbeck and the —'

'You're spilling the wine,' his father said. 'Sit down, I say, and hold your foolish tongue.'

Medley slid on to the bench beside his mother, but his eyes were all for the stranger.

'Your health, Kit,' Dick Plashet said. 'You've been a fine long while coming to visit.'

'I was forever promising I'd find you out. But you're skilled at hiding. And let's say nothing occurred that made it an urgent matter.'

Medley was sure, then, that someone had left his father a great fortune, and Master Crespin had brought the news—perhaps even gold in his saddlebags. They would be able to go to Ghylls Hatch and buy two fine horses from the scores bred there—no, three horses, for his mother must have some sturdy little beast that would match her stature.

'There need be no urgency in any meeting between us, Kit,' he heard his father saying. 'There can be none. You know that. It can't have been easy, finding out this place. I thought you did it for love.'

'I've been many months about it, if the truth's told. And of course it was for love, Richard, so don't glower. All news from the world, however, is bound to be one of two things—and *you* know *that*!'

'As—?'

'As an invitation, Richard Plashet—how that name reminds me of another—or as a warning . . .'

At once, as if some danger had entered by the door, there was such a feeling in the room it was as though lightning must strike. Medley almost flinched and he ducked his head slightly without knowing he had done it.

'Master Crespin brings riddles with him, Dick,' he heard his mother say. Her voice was low and shook a little, he thought it was with anger. 'Come you, Melly,' she said. 'Let you and me leave 'em to their talk.' She rose and went at once to the door and out of the

house, and he was bound to follow. He was bitterly
reluctant, for all that strange sensation that some threat
had been made as they sat together at table. He longed
to hear more, to listen to talk of London, to learn something of a world that was as far from him as heaven itself—
and perhaps to cudgel some sense out of the hints and
the riddles. Even when he was out of doors he would
have crept back to crouch on the threshold and listen,
only his mother gave him a shove, her firm small hand
hard between his shoulder-blades. 'Do as I bid,' she said
sharply. 'Bring your eyes and your ears along with
you. There's better things to see and hear than men's
talk.'

'Show 'em, then,' muttered the boy. He sounded as
sullen and cheated as he felt. She flicked him a glance
as if she would scold, then changed her mind. It might
be that she knew even better than he did how fear had
suddenly loomed over the wine cups a few seconds back,
and knew that he was afraid still, though uncertain why.

'Time I walked over to see how your grandfather's
doing. I'll need some company and he'll be glad to see
you.'

'Then Master Crespin'll be off and I'll not see him
again.'

'And a riddance to him, I'd say. Don't you go snudging
along that way, Melly. Lift your head up and walk
steady.'

'I walked this way twice today a'ready,' he grumbled.

'Well, fair going never harmed a body.'

And it was fair going. The long forest track mounted
between the trees, then swept round between heathery
banks and on across cleared ground. From the highest
point up there the downs could be seen to southward,
holding back the ocean. The sun was now almost down

but the heat remained behind. The ground had broken
down into fine white sand through which Medley shuffled
stupidly in his disappointed bad temper. The heather had
coloured brilliantly over the past week, not the early pink
bells that soon turned brown, but the true sharp purple
that most attracted the bees; they were working now in
a last noisy effort before going home. Already the ash
trees were bright with berry. It had been a good summer
and crops of every kind were full and fine. Medley tugged
a pair of cobnuts off the last hazel bush he passed, tore
off their green jackets and bit at the pale shell. But the
kernel was so small and milky it was not worth the trouble
of chewing.

'Three weeks an' more for those,' his mother said.
'Don't waste 'em. There's a tidy shatter of blackberries
to pick, and elder. When you're out of school t'morrer
and after, you'll best get picking.'

'I'm out of school this day, mother. I never did get
a chance to tell. Sir James, he closed school just after
noon, and we're not to go for lessons again till a fortnight.'

'That's good, then. Sir James knows there's a deal to
do this time o' year.'

'It's a holiday, mother! Roger and me's to go fishing
and such things.'

'There's time for all,' she said calmly. 'You shall get
your fishing, surelye. And I'll get my berries!' She
stopped dead and caught his arm. 'Look there!'

'It's that hart that's short an antler,' Medley said.
'There he goes! There! Taking the river—see him?'

They stood to watch the deer leap a narrow stream,
then bound up the far bank and head away towards the
nearest copse. The sight was so pretty it made Medley
grin with pleasure, and his bad temper oozed out of him.

'No more than a week's feed on him,' he said, in the voice of an expert. 'Let him grow, he'll be worth the poaching.'

Anis looked sideways at him and laughed. 'And would you poach him?'

'Someone could.'

'Leave it to someone, then.' She had a great tenderness for animals and would not so much as skin a rabbit for the pot. She had told Medley how the slaughter of coneys for their pelts, at Mantlemass when she was a child, had been to her a horror from which she had fled weeping, hiding herself until it was all over. This had left her with a strange compulsion to protect all fur and feather, and hoof and paw. It was not altogether reasonable, for she, like any other, ate meat when it was to be come by. She kept the cat comfortably indoors, which was fool-hardy when folks set such store by witchcraft. 'Now I see you feel your easy self again,' she said to the boy. 'It was the hart did it.'

'I wanted to hear the talk,' Medley complained. 'They'd be nabbling of Lunnon, and I did want to hear.'

'A load of rubbish, like as not. You forget Master Crespin now, Melly. He'll be gone when we get home, and that'll be no loss.'

'He'll come again, surelye?'

'Why would he? Did you ever see him before this time?'

'My father did. They talk like dear friends.'

'I'm all jawled out wi' talk of Master Crespin,' his mother said sharply. 'Let him go.'

They had come within sight of Mantlemass, where Medley's grandfather, Tom Bostel, who had been reeve to the last owner, lived in one of the cottages belonging to the manor. He was a man in his late sixties, vigorous in mind and heart, but crippled in both legs since an accident last year when they were cutting beech for building. His youngest daughter, Peg, looked after him, for his wife had been dead some years.

Peg Bostel was pulling the washing off the line as her sister and Medley came up the track to the cottage. Peg was tall and thin, with a pale face that was nearly beautiful but her cold sharp eyes spoilt it. His mother had told Medley that Peg was dissatisfied with her life, and unhappy, and this made her hard. When she saw them coming towards her, Peg bundled the clean linen into the skep and went straight indoors.

'There she go,' said Medley. His mother said, 'Aye,' and left it at that, but he felt her stiffen as she walked beside him and it made him move nearer to her, so that he seemed to stand at her shoulder. She looked at him and smiled. They were almost of a height, but that would not last much longer. The balance was already on his side. Since about last month he had found that he could look down on her if he stretched his neck a bit.

They went into the cottage, and there was his grandfather sitting by the hearth with a rag rug over his poor legs. Of all his children he seemed to love this daughter best—perhaps because she was like her mother, for whom she had been named Anis, and because his marriage had been a very contented one.

'Bless you, father,' she said as she entered. 'I brought Medley to see how you do. Sir James sent the lads out of school. For this whole week and next, he tell me. That's a good time, for I've work for twenty.'

'Set him to it, then,' said Tom, chuckling. 'What's childer for? Don't you be hang-dog, now, Melly. I dunnamuch store your mother set by you. Heed her.'

'I do,' said Medley sullen.

'Call Peg, Anis,' Tom Bostel said. 'She'll pour you a cup of ale. It's hot weather and a dusty walk.'

'No matter, father,' said Anis. 'Leave her be. Medley and me, we come to see you, not Peg.'

'What's between you?' he muttered. 'We never had no quarrels among us till now.'

'Peg's had a quarrel with me these long year, and that you well know, father. And know why. And if Ned and John or any of the rest were here now, they'd have a quarrel with me, too. And you and me, father, we both know why.'

'I'll hear no ill of you, my girl.'

'Thank you, father,' said Anis. She looked at Medley thoughtfully, as if she wondered whether he knew what they were talking about. 'You go to the big house, Melly,' she ordered him. 'Ask for Dame Cecily. Say I've that soothing salve half brewed that she asked me for— but t'idn't ready yet.'

Medley went at once, glad of release. The day which had seemed so easy and pleasant at its start was now made complex by hints and riddles. These formed themselves into a bubble of unease within his mind, and the bubble would not burst and so be dispersed, but all the time swelled larger, becoming ugly as it grew. He was ready to run the errand but it proved fruitless, for Dame Cecily and all the rest had gone to Ghylls Hatch on some business about horses. Ghylls Hatch belonged to Master Roger Orlebar, who was Roger Mallory's godfather. Roger would inherit Ghylls Hatch one day—a far finer thing, so Medley always thought, than to be heir to Mantlemass itself—that would go to Simon, the elder son.

Medley hung about the rickyard, where they were still thatching, though the light was dwindling. Simon Mallory had gone with the rest to Ghylls Hatch and lanky Davy was in charge of the thatching now. He grinned down at Medley and said it was a sore shame how some lads never did a hand's turn. He spoke so thickly and stutteringly that no one could understand him that did not know him well. Still, he had got himself a pretty, silly wife, who giggled the days away, and two round pink children, with another on the way—so he was a happy man.

There was no one for miles around—these Mantlemass people, and all the rest over at Ghylls Hatch, the charcoal burners and the furnace men, the men at the forges and the farms, the village women, and all those who were a part of forest life—whom Medley could not call by name. Yet he was aware, this last year or so since he began to think a bit, that he was not entirely absorbed among them. He was closest, indeed, to those furthest above him—only with the Mallorys was he altogether himself, free and without reserve, his mother still a part of the place, Roger Mallory his dearest friend. Perhaps it was his father's curious pride, the fact that he was a stranger and seemed willing to remain so, that raised a nameless barrier between him and the rest, and this attached to his family. And then, once, coldly and in some terror, Medley had wondered if his mother's skill with herbs and medicines, and her reckless tenderness for animals, had set tongues wagging with talk of witchcraft. There was none she had tended that had not benefited from her care, but strange things could happen—and one day he saw a village woman, who had been gathering acorns, cross herself as she passed the cottage door.

Medley hung about the rickyard now with the dusk coming down, and no one passed without giving him a greeting. The master and mistress of the place had a name for courtesy and hospitality through all that countryside, and their people seemed to have learnt from them. When he was done with school Medley planned to ask for work here. He could have been working for at least three years, like scores of other lads, but his father had kept him to his lessons. Not that he was expected or allowed to be idle at home. He had gathered kindling since he was six years old, and now he chose and chopped tougher stuff, making a pile against the cottage wall to last the winter. In the bit of pasture the old horse shared summer quarters with the little brown cow, and it was for Medley to see both fed and watered and the cow milked when his mother was too busy. Sometimes he had to sneak out if he wanted to go jaunting with Roger. One way and another he had plenty to do and plenty to think about—as now he was thinking, while he loitered, of Master Crespin and the strange things that had been said. What had been said about his own name, for instance, about his fortunes being a medley—and that moment when danger had seemed to loom out of nowhere, to threaten as they sat quietly at the table . . .

By the time Medley returned to his grandfather's his mother was outside looking for him.

'They are all gone to Ghylls Hatch. I couldn't give any message.'

'That's a tidy while to take not giving it! Come on along home. It'll be dark any time.'

This time as they walked the familiar track, Anis was silent. In spite of the dusk, the last bees were still at the heather, and there was a red-breast singing as they came near home and looked towards the far bank where great trees began. That song meant the ending of summer, but it would carry them through the winter days. It was like a thread tying the two ends of the year together.

Anis checked suddenly and made a sharp clucking

sound of annoyance. Master Crespin was only just leaving; he and Dick Plashet still had something to say to one another, it seemed—something that must be said even though it took till near-dark. Through the increasing dusk, Medley saw Master Crespin hold out both hands in farewell, and then, quite unexpectedly, the two men embraced like brothers. Crespin mounted and Dick looked up at him and smiled, and gave the fine horse an affectionate slap on the flank. Master Crespin laughed as the animal sprang forward. He held it in firmly, turning again as at last he began to move off, to hold up his hand in final farewell. He called something that Medley could not properly hear, and he followed it with a roar of laughter.

'What'd he say?' Medley asked his mother.

'Some jest,' she answered flatly. 'A Lunnon jest your father tell me of once. They'd mock Dick Plashet and call him Richard Plantagenet. Master Crespin called it out—God keep you, Richard Plantagenet. That's a king's name—your father was said to favour him in looks. He was the King afore our King Henry—killed in battle, they say.'

'Oh surelye!' Medley cried impatiently. 'Anyone know that. Bosworth Field, mother—when the wars ended. I don't see what make you so miffed.'

'Miffed? Am I? Let's say I don't like Lunnon talk. He'll be reminded of all those days. Best forgotten, ask me.' She looked at Medley and said slowly and quietly, 'Come you love someone, you do burn with jealousy of them as knew him first.'

Master Crespin had now caught sight of Medley and his mother approaching through the twilight. He swung his horse down the bank and took the stream, pulling up beside them.

'I'll not leave without a farewell, Dame Anis. And you,
Medley boy—remember me in your prayers from time
to time.'

He looked so splendid with the last primrose light of
the sky behind him, sitting his grand horse in his fine
clothes, that Medley was quite dazzled. Truly he knew
in his heart that his father was no plain forester, no
ordinary guide or builder, though he acted as any of these
and lived no other way. But it was quite amazing that he
should have such a friend as this grand gentleman.

'It's late, sir,' the boy said, desperately bold. 'Will you
stay till morning?'

'No, I must travel tonight.'

'Then—will you come again?'

'Maybe. Remember—I will always be there to show
you London when you come?' His horse had stopped
beside a bush of broom which showed two or three small
yellow blooms, as often happened at this time of year.
Master Crespin stooped out of his saddle and pulled off
two pieces of the broom, each of which had one blossom.
He stuck one in his doublet and held out the other to
Medley. 'Keep that for me.'

'This, sir?'

'Aye—the sprig of broom. Keep it for me.' He laughed
again and called 'Farewell!' then spurred his horse and
cantered away down the track without a backward glance.

'All Lunnon men be mad,' Anis said. 'Throw it away
and come indoors.'

She walked away at once, as though she felt so impatient
of these madmen she could not brush them off her
shoulders fast enough.

Medley hesitated a second. He did not want to throw
away Master Crespin's strange token. He thought first of
slipping it inside his shirt and taking it indoors without

his mother knowing. But it would soon wither and have to be thrown away. There must be some way of keeping it, as Master Crespin had told him to.

'Medley!' his mother called.

He bent quickly and stuck the sprig into the ground in the shade of its parent by the stream. That way he would look at it for a week or so before it withered, and he would think of Master Crespin and of London, where his father had been as a lad and learnt his trade as apprentice to a master builder—and been teased by his fellow apprentices, just as Medley himself might be. Though how he had ever become friends with Master Crespin was hard to see—for he had surely never been any tradesman's apprentice.

4
Encounter

In fine autumn weather Medley and Roger Mallory fished
hopefully along the little river below Mantlemass. They
were free of lessons because Sir James was sick and kept
to his bed. Everyone knew without speaking of it that he
was likely to die; he was a very old man.

It was mid-October, the harvest well stored. The sun
was as hot as if it shone in the first week of September,
but a tumbling sky threw great clouds before the wind,
and when the sun was obscured then all the promise of
winter was in the air. But it was magic weather, a gift
to sweeten the sadness of the ending year. There were
still blackberries, thick and dripping with juice, but these

4

would remain on the bushes, for by now, as it was said, the Devil had spat on them and they should not be eaten. So birds gorged themselves, and the ground and the leaves of the brambles were strewn with purple droppings. The water, half shadow and half glitter, threw back the colours of beech and bracken, tossing them over the boulders like gold and copper coins.

The boys had no luck with their fishing, and the warmth of the afternoon drowsed silently over the narrow secret place as the two of them lolled on the bank with scarcely energy to speak. Medley lay on his stomach, staring down into the water until it lulled him almost into a dream. Then he thought he saw something move in the bushes opposite, and at once he was alert, expecting deer. No animal emerged, yet Medley knew that there was something there. His flesh prickled slightly. He put his hand out slowly to twitch at Roger's sleeve. Hardly breathing, he said, 'Someone watching.'

Roger was lying on his back with his arms behind his head. He could be relied upon to behave suitably, and he rolled over slowly and silently. His lips barely moved as he replied, 'Certain?'

'Mm.'

'Davy said there were strangers riding by Ghylls Hatch yesterday . . .'

There was a slithering sound opposite and both boys sprang as far as their knees in readiness for whatever action might need to be taken.

'It's my sister,' Roger said in disgust, as young Catherine slid down the far bank, feet first into the water. 'You spying sneak, Puss Mallory. How long've you been there listening?'

'An hour, I'd say, and nothing worth hearing.'

'We don't talk private matters where girls can listen.'

'She's a lad again today,' Medley corrected him. 'She's got on the hose you promised me.'

'Where's your gown, madam?' demanded Roger, in their brother Simon's most gentlemanly voice. And then, because she spluttered into laughter, he had to laugh, too, and Medley joined in. Catherine looked relieved. She splashed through the water and clambered to the bank, sitting at three paces' distance, hugging her knees and curling her bare toes and looking pleased with herself. 'Puss-cat,' said Roger, 'you're too old for these antics. It's time you learnt some maidenly modesty. I'm fearing that Medley's blushing to see you.'

'I am not,' growled Medley. He looked at her and grinned. Her hair had been cropped short in the spring when she had had a bad fever, and now it curled gently on her neck and on her brow. It was a fine pale gold colour, with a hint almost of green—most like to the silk round the husks of maize—the same colour as her mother's was still. Medley wondered if Dame Cecily knew that the girl was out in her brother's clothes again. Possibly so, for the lady of Mantlemass had an easy-going way with her that quite scandalised some of the neighbours. Certainly the women in the village, inclined to think themselves above rough foresty ways, were *nonplushed*, as they said, when a lady was so free, and so lacking in rebuke of her children, laughing more than she scolded and never lifting a hand against them. Medley had heard his own mother say in defence of such easy manners, that Dame Cecily had learnt from her aunt, Dame Elizabeth FitzEdmund, who had been lady of Mantlemass before her.

'Have you any fish?' asked Catherine, placating her brother by a show of interest. 'Shall we make a fire and cook 'em? I can make a fire, for Davy learned me.'

'Davy taught you, my dear sister,' said Roger.

'And that's what I said he done—'

'—did . . .'

'Yes . . . You must put exactly the right sticks exactly the right way, and done so it will burn many hours. It will be a hot fiery pudding . . . So shall I make it?'

'There's no fish to cook. Cursed poor sport we've had,' said Roger. And he spat in a swaggering way to show his disgust.

'Looks you must keep your hot fiery pudding,' said Medley.

'Shall I not make it to warm our hands?'

'Shall she, Roger?'

Roger stirred himself at last. 'Run you home, Puss, and beg some bread and meat from the kitchen. Do that and you shall have your fire and roast the meat for us.'

The girl scrambled up the bank and was gone almost before her brother had finished speaking. They saw her go pelting off up the track, her bare feet grimy from the dry, dusty ground, her legs sunburned to the colour of good oak.

Roger looked after her and grinned. 'She makes a good enough little brother.'

'It'll go sore hard the day she must turn lady,' Medley said.

'Nor it cannot be so long till then, Melly. She's all but twelve years old.'

'Lord, if I'd been born a female I'd sooner be dead!' cried Medley, shuddering. 'I would that, Roger Mallory. Sooner be dead than tripping over a gown and sitting my horse sideways, the way ladies do.'

And Medley sat shaking his head over the hard lot of women, and thanking God piously for his own good fortune, till Roger lost patience. He struck out and punched so hard that Medley overbalanced and went

rolling down the bank into the river. 'Hang you!' he
bellowed, as Roger followed him down and pushed him
back into the water as fast as he struggled out. They
tussled and struck at one another, shouting and laughing
—but indeed only just laughing. At last Medley swung
up both feet as he lay on his back in the shallow water,
planted them neatly against Roger's stomach and sent him
backward in his turn. They were still splashing and
roaring when Catherine returned.

'You should've had bavins gathered for the fire!' she
scolded. 'Get out of that water, you lazy runagates!'

They were glad to obey and emerged as fast as they
could. Roger's hose were soaked and the back of his
leather jerkin black with wet. Medley had fared worse
in an old doublet cut down from one of his father's, thick
enough to hold the wet but not thick enough to keep it
out. Water was trickling nastily down his back.

'Take off your doublet,' Catherine ordered. 'The fire
shall soon dry it.'

Medley hesitated. Beneath his doublet he wore a shirt
so often mended that it barely held together, and he
knew he had rent it badly in his fight with Roger; also
he had his hose tied up with a bit of cord because the
points were worn out.

'I'll be cold without it,' he said, holding the soaking
wet doublet closer to his chest.

'You'll be shivering and roupy come sundown if you
stay soused as you are,' she said roughly. 'Hang it on
the bushes till I get the fire going.'

Slowly and reluctantly, Medley did as he was bidden.
He tugged the wet sleeves over his hands and at long
last peeled the doublet off his back. Standing in his
torn shirt and shabby old hose, he felt ashamed. Roger
was paying no attention, he was gathering up sticks for

the fire—but Catherine stood waiting, holding out her hand for the wet doublet like anybody's scolding mother. He felt himself blushing, his poverty being so baldly displayed, and he pulled the torn shirt across his shoulders, holding the rents together hopefully. He looked apologetically at Catherine. She was a curious enough figure herself, with her sheared-off hose, and doublet two sizes too big, and her manner only a minute before had been as brusque and forthright as any lad's. But looking at him now she was entirely changed. She was half smiling, not in mockery, but with a warmth and compassion far beyond her years. For a fleeting moment he thought how fine it would be if she were his sister, not Roger's, that he might hug her close and thank her for her soft understanding. But the thought was dead as soon as it was born. He did not want her for a sister—one day he would need a wife and only Puss Mallory would do. And that thought, too, was so wild it must go the way of the first—for he would certainly never get her. Shabby little creature as she looked at the moment, she was highly connected and not for any foresty lad.

As he handed over his wet doublet, Medley felt a great helplessness and despair—as though he were already grown and denied for ever his only hope of happiness . . .

Catherine shook out the doublet and squeezed the water out busily, chattering as she did so as if she would pretend she had never looked so sweetly and so kindly at him. Yet the chatter itself was full of understanding.

'It'll take time to dry, surelye,' she said. 'It's heavy as lead with the wet. It's a fine doublet, too. Was it ever your father's? My brother Simon can wear our father's doublets now without ever any cutting or stitching. This is fine, fine cloth, Medley, and bravely sewn. Did it come from Lunnon, think you? London, I mean. My nurse Meg tell me your father come from London before you was ever born. Was it so?'

'And has friends in Lunnon to this day,' boasted Medley. 'One come only last month and talked with him, and sat down very grateful at our own table. A gentleman. He had the finest horse in the kingdom—save those at Ghylls Hatch,' he added quickly, seeing her open her mouth to protest. 'So even if my father do be a man of trades, he has grand friends.'

'He is a mysterious man,' Catherine said, spreading the doublet over a bush and pulling at the creases. 'Mysterious,' she repeated, drawing out the word as if she enjoyed it. 'Melly Plashet has a mysterious father.'

'You make it sound sinful, almost!'

'Oh no! Mysteries are like ballads and poems and stories with the wrong endings.' But when he challenged her she could not explain what *wrong endings* were.

Roger had built the fire while they were talking, but then there was no way to light it, and he sent his sister running to the house again. She came back walking very slowly, holding in both hands the little old-fashioned stable lantern, that was kept always burning. It had a bowl of oil that swung as it was carried, and the flame flickered and dipped as the level of oil in the bowl adjusted to the movement; but the invention was not perfect and the oil slopped and splashed.

'Take care with it!' Roger cried. 'You know it should not be moved from its place. Mind what you're about— do you want to set the whole forest a-blaze?'

He sounded so angry that she faltered, looking down at the dangerous flame for the first time—as a climber on a rock face will look down and then know terror. A spurt of hot oil in fact slopped from the lamp and fell to the ground, and Catherine sprang back to save her bare foot. She stepped on to a tuft of yellow furze, and tried to avoid that. She overbalanced, then, and at last went full length and began slithering down the bank.

'Catch her, you fool!' yelled Roger.

Catherine screamed. The dangerous little lantern had fallen from her hands as she tried to save herself, and it rolled ahead of her, spilling flaring oil as it went. In the seconds it took her to roll and slither and struggle on the bank, the flame had licked at the oil that had spilled on her clothes, and run over one bare foot.

Roger was trying to tear off his jerkin, but the lacing was too wet to undo. Medley's doublet still hung on the bush and he seized it as he sprang by and hurled himself down the bank. It was only another second or two before he had flung the doublet over Catherine, heavy with wet as it was, and exactly fitted for the crisis. She was moaning and shivering and he tried to pick her up and carry her back up the bank, but it was too steep. Roger was beating out the fire that threatened to spread and cut a way into the bushes, shouting as he did so, 'I said you shouldn't have brought it! What did you expect?' But his fury covered his alarm for his sister and his own feeling of guilt—it was he who had sanctioned the fire. 'Are you badly hurt?' he cried, as he helped Medley get her up the bank. 'Are you much burned?'

'Don't bawl so, you chucklehead!' Medley snapped. 'It's bad enough without your shouting!' He hung over Catherine as if only he could protect her, and protect her from the whole world.

'You're stifling her,' Roger said, more sensibly now the fire was out. 'Bring her home.'

'It hurts!' she wailed. 'Oh, Melly—oh, Melly, it does hurt so!'

Medley wished with all his heart that they had been

nearer his home than hers, for his mother would know what to do. But Dame Cecily had always gone to Anis for her salves and medicines so maybe the right preparation was already at Mantlemass. He tucked the wet doublet more tidily round Catherine and began to carry her up the track. Her foot was bright red and already showing blisters. Suppose it had been her face and she had been scarred for ever . . . With a burst of wisdom, he thought strangely and clearly that then they might have been glad to let him marry her. It was a wild way to think about a child still young enough to enjoy dressing up as a boy . . .

'We'll take turns carrying her,' Roger said.

'Grab tight round my neck,' Medley ordered Catherine. He would carry her all the way, he thought, and her mother would thank him, and remember . . .

In her distress Dame Cecily had few thanks to give.

'Your father shall pay you for this, Roger! Bring her this way—this way. God save us all, are you so little to be trusted with a child? If it weren't for your mother, Medley Plashet, I'd see you well beaten before you set out for home!' She was whirling ahead of him through the hall, her skirts slapping fold on fold, and five or so women ran and chattered about her. Her fists were clenched and she was as pale as her own linen with rage and alarm. Her eyes, Medley said afterwards, struck sparks whatever they lighted upon. She was a beautiful and gentle woman but now she was like a tempest and the two boys quailed at the thunder of the unfamiliar threats she summoned up. 'I'll have you shut up on bread and water for this! Nay—I'll see you starving, both! Meg—fetch the blue jar from my closet. Tear me some linen, one of you women. There, there, my poor Kitten—you shall soon be well!'

'Mother! Mother!' wailed Catherine. 'Oh, my foot—my foot! Oh, I do so burn!'

'Gently, gently. Meg is fetching the salve. The pain will go, I promise. Bring her to the settle, Medley. There now—there. Now go—and let my son go with you before I set about him with my own bare hands.'

'It were Medley save me,' Catherine said faintly. Even then, she corrected herself as if she thought Roger would do so otherwise. 'It was Medley who saved me, madam, and put his wet doublet round me. Pray you, never send him away!'

Medley looked fearfully at Dame Cecily. And she paused and looked at him. He saw her gaze suddenly accepting him—his torn shirt, his raggedy hose, his shabbiness that matched his wild look of anxiety and self-reproach. The anger seemed to fly away out of her like some evil and unfamiliar spirit. Then Meg, who had long served in that house, and been nurse to all Dame Cecily's children, returned with the blue jar.

'Your mother gave me this salve, Medley,' Dame Cecily said in a low voice. 'So it will be she who makes my daughter whole again.' She half smiled at him. 'Now go, child. Roger, go with him. Give him something of yours to wear or he'll take a chill. Meg and the rest of us will see to your sister.'

The two boys left the chamber. As they went one of the women said to another—'That were Dame Elizabeth's mantle our lady wore then. Voice and all. Like a sign from the dead, Mary.' Then Catherine began to cry as her mother touched her scorched skin, and Medley went quickly through the door and sat down.

'I must tell thee, Melly,' Roger said, sitting beside him, 'that none could have acted quicker or braver. I shouted for fear, not anger.'

'Yes,' agreed Medley.

'And now,' said Roger, 'we're more than ever brothers.'

He had never said openly before that they were any sort of brother, and Medley's heart almost burst with the force and confusion of his feelings. He would willingly have sworn fealty to Roger as to a liege lord; to be his brother—to be his *more than ever* brother—was like some fine dream of chivalry come true.

Medley walked home carrying the blue salve-jar, which his mother must fill again for Dame Cecily. Meg had brought the jar to him, and she had said her young lady was not so badly hurt as all that—she would soon be well. And though it was certainly their fault, his and Roger's—for Meg would never blame a girl if there was a boy to bear the brunt—none the less they had acted quickly and cleverly in getting the poor child home so fast, and in seeing, too, that the fire was out before it should spread. 'Now take this to your mother, boy, and be certain sure to bring it back filled afore night. The burns must be dressed again last thing of all. So no doddling.'

Medley did not doddle. It would be dark before he made his fourth journey of that day between home and Mantlemass. He was used enough to the forest at night and knew his way so well he reckoned he could escape any danger less than lightning striking from heaven. He could not see in the dark but nor could he be seen. The dusk always seemed to him more frightening, with the shadows so deep and the shapes so strange—the most familiar bush or tree could seem to menace at dusk. Not that there were many dangers to fear. There were outlaws of one sort or another about the forest, but they mostly kept to themselves. When they plundered it was farther afield—they existed in two or three small bands whose numbers fluctuated, and they would make sorties about the countryside when they were in need. It was to their advantage to stay friends with the foresters, who would need provocation to inform on them—it was an unwritten promise that fugitives were to be treated as comrades. The laws of the forest concerning game and the use of land and timber, which belonged to the King, made every forester an outlaw of a kind, taking his life in his hands for a haunch of meat or a new rafter. So it was less any human threat that could cause Medley to look over his shoulder quickly as he went about the forest at twilight, than the goblins and spirits of his childhood which existed still for him at such times.

Between Mantlemass and Plashet's there was a broad clearing where lived Rufus Goodale and his three old sisters. Rufus lived by the trade of guiding; it was from him that Dick Plashet had learnt how best to conduct strangers through the forest. The landlord of the inn up on the road that led eventually into London would send a boy running to Rufus Goodale when strangers asked for help, and Rufus then sent to one or another of those he had trained up. He kept a few rather worn-out horses as a part of his trade, and these were a constant bone of contention with the Ghylls Hatch people, whose fine horses had half their quality from the care with which they were bred up from foals. Master Lewis Mallory, who had become lord of Mantlemass when his wife's aunt died, had been brought up at Ghylls Hatch. Medley had learnt from the Mallorys to look with some passion upon the right treatment of horses—he was often ashamed of his father's thin beast. He looked instinctively for Goodale's animals as he went across the clearing, but none was to be seen.

At this time of year, men moved on journeys that must

be made before winter set in, and the guides were in some demand. Though it was no longer likely that any man would need a series of sixteen guides to see him from end to end of the forest, the place was still dense and dangerous and covered a vast area of the countryside. It had many bogs, old mine pits and stone quarries, all overgrown and terrible traps for the unwary.

One of Rufus's sisters, Deb Goodale, came out as Medley passed carrying the blue salve-jar, his mind seething with thoughts of knightly brotherhood and the winning of his chosen lady; and wondering if he might tell such matters to his mother, who had never laughed yet at any confidence, however wild.

Old Deb called out to Medley, waving to him across the shadowy clearing. 'Your father's from home.' She had a beard almost as fine as her brother's and was thought by some, though without much malice, to be a witch. 'My brother send for him late after noon. There's travellers to be led for the coast.'

'So late?'

'All of five past noon when they set out, and then must find a third of their company—he was about the place I know not where. Your father were in a high old lash afore they left—he don't take mildly to such pestering. You should know that, I dessay.'

'He's proud,' said Medley, feeling proud himself. But pride was not truly excuse enough for a man obliged to scratch a living.

'You'll come up with 'em even now, I shouldn't wonder,' old Deb called after him, for he was in no mood for lingering over gossip. 'Coastwise, I said. One had a shoe loose, after all that boffle, and they must go first to the forge.'

In spite of his preoccupation, Medley did feel curious,

for so many delays and annoyances would certainly have put his father into a fine rage. He sloped off at the next fork and began to clamber on a deer-run that led him up steep ground. From the top he would look over several miles of heathland, and he had seen fine stags standing to survey the ground from that vantage point.

The moment he reached the summit Medley came out of the trees and the shadows. The sky was clear, lifted into immensity by the chilly primrose light flushing up from the west and spreading to touch the farthest eastern horizon. Distant trees, single bushes, rocks, appeared in this light a deep rich purple with outlines sharp and hard as iron. And Deb Goodale had been right, for almost as Medley looked out from the high ground, three strangers came into view, and with them his father.

Medley had expected, if indeed he was to see them at all, to watch them riding briskly towards the south-east for they had lost much time, and would surely need to reach the downs before the dark came properly down. But the scene was quite different. The four men moved close together, and at a walk. He heard their voices, which rose urgently, even angrily, then dropped and seemed to wheedle. The three strangers were close in round Dick Plashet. They appeared to menace him, yet he remained apparently calm. By many signs, Medley knew that his father was deeply angry, though it would not be seen by any who did not know him well. He sat very straight on his horse, taut and contained; but then he made a wide sharp gesture of the arm that Medley had often seen—as though he would sweep all that hindered and pestered him clean from his path.

Even the primrose light was now fading, and Medley had to strain his eyes to watch. The voices, quarrelsome and insistent, grew increasingly confused. He could not separate one word from another, until at last his father's studied calm broke up in a great shout of fury: 'I have answered you—and for the last time! Be it understood, then. The last time!'

He heeled out of the press and turned his horse as if he would ride away and abandon them. Now their shouts were easier to hear. 'Wait!' 'You are bound to guide us!' 'We'll break our necks if you quit us now!'

Medley began to pelt along the flat top of his bank, for he knew if he went fast he would see them again where they plunged into the trees before taking the right turn round a stretch of marshy land. He emerged just in time and ran out into open ground. He did not quite know what he intended, but he was sure his father needed some help and must benefit by knowing there was at least someone who had seen and heard them quarrelling. Perhaps, exalted by the events of the day, feeling twice his size because he was Roger Mallory's *more than ever* brother, he saw himself as his father's rescuer and protector. The instant the horses came into view, he dashed forward.

'Master!' he shouted—for many of the boys he knew addressed their fathers in this style. 'Where are you bound, master?'

The horsemen reined in as sharply as if a hobgoblin had sprung from the shadows, and the horses pranced a bit.

'Who's this?' one of the strangers asked. 'Who's this, then, Richard?'

His father looked down casually at Medley, his face quite blank and indifferent.

'The lads hereabouts are forever begging rides,' he said. 'Out of the way, boy. We're short enough of time as it is.'

Medley stepped back. He might as well have had a bough break over his head. He was stunned. Indeed he stepped so carelessly that he went into a rut and over-balanced, falling back flat. Dick Plashet dug in his heels and his horse leapt forward. For a second Medley thought he must be ridden into the ground, and he flung up one arm to cover his face. His father was past in a flash, and the strangers moved after him, but the last held his horse and called out, 'What's your name?'

'Medley—sir.'

'Well, Tom, or Dick, or Harry Medley—you seem to know our guide.'

'Foresters knows foresters,' Medley answered, and he made it a growl. His voice was rougher than he would have dared let his father hear it. 'I bluv he'm the most masterful guide, and all know'un. He do a dezzick more powerful than any else.'

'Lord help us,' said the stranger, 'as well be overseas as understand you folk.'

The others now shouted back at him to hurry. The gentleman tossed his head and lifted up his eyes as if he could hardly believe such uncouth creatures as this boy existed in the same world as he inhabited. He shook up his horse and moved off.

Soon the horses were out of sight, swallowed by the shadowy trees ahead, and the ground upon which Medley lay no longer carried the message of their passing. All was still save Medley's heart and mind, as he rolled over on to his face and thrust it into the heather. It was as though he had long expected this encounter without ever daring to tell himself it could happen. He lay absolutely still, remembering many things he had wanted to thrust away from him. Such as his father's strangeness, his difference from all the rest, his way of speech that was

from another mode of life, his reserve that could be gentle
or cold as winter. How he had said to Master Crespin
His fortunes are a medley . . . Then he thought of his
aunt, Peg Bostel, who would not speak to her sister, and
of what his mother had said that day at his grandfather's
home, his grandfather saying *I'll hear no ill of you,
girl* . . . These things gushed and roared in Medley's
mind. He thought how he had known for some time that
he never heard his mother say as the other women did
That were before I wed . . . How she always called Dick
Plashet *master*, as Medley had just done, and never
addressed him as *husband* . . . As he came to this point
Medley was bound to face what had been shifting in his
mind for a long while, but he had not wanted to admit
it—that all these things were because Anis and Dick
Plashet were not man and wife, but lived together in
defiance of the laws of the land and of the church. This,
he thought, was why his father would not acknowledge
him in front of the strangers—because he was a child
born out of wedlock. It meant that he had no rights and
never would have—that it was nonsense to think of himself as Roger Mallory's brother, either in the way of
friendship or as a match for his sister. Medley flushed
and burned with humiliation as he recalled those bold
ideas for the future that had taken his mind and his
imagination only a few hours ago. He had always thought
Dame Cecily was good to him because she was fond of
him and his mother; now he was sure she merely pitied
him, and perhaps so did Roger . . . But this idea was
so base he knew it was not true and he rejected it; Roger
was too blunt to be clever in deception.

Medley lay a long time with his face in the heather,
but he could not hide for ever. He rolled over at last,
remembering that he must take the salve-jar and get it

5

filled, and run with it again to Mantlemass for Catherine's
sake. The jar had fallen to the ground and the lid was
off. Neither was broken, but he had to start groping
about in the dark for the lid, and by the time he found
it he was snivelling and muttering in his wretchedness.
He picked up the lid and went home at a jog trot, pushing
away tears he had supposed himself too old to shed. The
shadows stood back to let him pass and there were ghouls
and goblins in every bush and tree. But he no longer
saw them. There were other things now for him to fear.
He thought he would never be plagued by mere shadows
ever again.

5
The Wrong Ending . . .

By noon next day Dick Plashet had not returned. Medley had said nothing to his mother of the encounter. She had seen his distress when he got home, but this had seemed reasonable as he had such a tale to tell of the afternoon's affairs.

'I recall that very lamp,' his mother said. 'The smith give it to Dame Elizabeth for a token at Christmas time. That were long ago and it were always a danger to touch. My brother Ned did take it once, and spilt it, and got a beating.' She smiled as she remembered her childhood. 'We played all about at Mantlemass,' she said, 'all the poorest and the best like one. So it were wi' the old

Dame, and so now with Dame Cecily and her good man.'

She was filling the blue jar with salve from a big pot, and the smell of sweet herbs was on the air. 'And then,' said Medley, watching her clean the horn spoon and seal the lid on the jar, 'there come my father out of London to work on building the new barn.' He slipped a quick look at her face, then back to her busy hands. 'And carried you off,' he said.

'Aye. Some new style of work and Master Lewis Mallory would have skilled men sent. That made some hereabout pretty vlothered, I can tell thee. I never heard a word spoke against Mantlemass except that time.'

Medley raised his head at that. 'So did they blame my father for it?'

'Some.'

A sudden hope rose up in Medley, that all his conjectures were false and here was the simple explanation of his father's cool treatment by the rest—that even his denial of his own son might be bound up here in some fashion he could not remotely understand. 'And is that why—' he blurted out. Then broke off because she was utterly still.

'Why what?'

'Sometime he do seem to be—he do seem to be no part of the forest.'

Anis did not answer this. She tied the seal on the jar and snipped the thread and said without looking at him, 'Best take it rightawaynow. Mind out how you go in the dark.' And at once she turned her back on him and threw wood on the fire.

He dared not speak again; he wished with all his heart he had held his tongue and never spoken. He went out of the door and ran through the dark to Mantlemass.

It was not until the next dusk that they heard the horse coming up the track. Anis had been boiling apples and honey to make a conserve, and now she was ready to pull the pan from the fire. She lifted her head as she heard the sound of hooves. She was always uneasy when Dick was from home, this time more than ever, Medley thought. Her shoulders relaxed.

'Go and take the horse,' she said.

Medley had gone to the open door, then turned sharply away. He stood by the window, staring out obliquely, as if he wished to see without being seen.

'Do as you're bid!' said Anis, suddenly sharp.

Medley went then. He was sick with fear at what might happen next, for last evening must be spoken of—if his father did not speak, then Medley must, for he could not accept what had happened without knowing the cause—he would rather go from his home and never return. He went outside. His father had just dismounted. The boy went forward and took the bridle without speaking and without looking.

He led the horse away to the field behind the cottage, took off the saddle and turned the creature loose. There was little grass at this time. He went into the meagre stable, a lean-to on the back wall, hung up the saddle on its peg and collected a panful of oats and an armful of hay. As he went out of the door again he seemed to see the saddle for the first time, and he turned back to look at it. It was of fine leather, well stitched and fashioned and polished with much use. It had belonged, no doubt, to that first horse of his father's, of which he had often been told, a creature beyond compare, named Sceptre. Now suddenly the saddle seemed an incongruous possession for a man scratching a living off the forest. How many of Rufus Goodale's guides owned any saddle at all?

Medley went on his way and fed the horse. He stood by the water trough watching it drink and thinking that it, too, could be a beast worthy of the saddle, if only it were better kept.

At last there was nothing more to keep him and he was obliged to leave the field and go into the house. The door was standing open as usual, the hens picking about the step and into the kitchen. Medley saw his father and mother standing just inside the door. His arm was round her and she had her cheek pressed against his shoulder.

'Why must you have such fears?' Medley heard his father say.

Anis answered, 'You well know why.' Then they moved apart as the boy approached. Anis turned back to the great pan she had pulled from the hearth and ladled the hot conserve into waiting crocks. 'Your father has rid a fine long way,' she said. 'Draw him a mug of ale.'

Medley took from the shelf the best pewter mug that his grandfather had given them, and carried it down to the cellar. He watched the ale bubble to a head under the spigot and seemed to be looking into an image of his own troubled mind. He heard voices while he was down below and when he came up again there was a young woman at the door. He knew her as the wife of one of the charcoal burners, living in a hovel half a mile or so away.

'The child's tissicking like a roupey old hen,' she was saying in a wheedling anxious voice. 'They did say there was none more than you who'd know what's best to do.'

Anis hesitated, looking at Dick. 'The master's just home and needs a bite,' she said.

'Go with her,' he said. 'Do what you can. Medley shall bear me company.'

Medley put down the ale. His mother slid two small phials and a pot of honey into her apron pockets, and took down her shawl. His father stood by the hearth watching her. He was waiting for her to be out of earshot, Medley knew. There was to be no dodging the issue. He had to face whatever was to come. He looked under his eyebrows at his father, almost as though he expected punishment. He longed to call to his mother to stay, to wait a little, to save him from what was to be said. She did glance back once and seemed to give him a half-smile—perhaps of encouragement. Then she followed after the young woman and the dusk swallowed her.

Instantly, as though he feared the briefest silence would be hard to break, Dick Plashet said, 'Ask me what you want to know. You have every right to question me.'

This was so unexpected that Medley's eyes filled with tears. He could not speak, but sat down at the table and laid his arm along the scrubbed boards and his head on his arm to hide his grief. He struggled to be firm. He pressed his lips together, but his bitter sorrow rose thickly into his throat and almost choked him.

'Well, then—I shall try to tell you why you should not hate me,' his father said. 'It is not certain you will understand, for I cannot tell you everything. There'd be no profit in that, even if I found it suitable.'

'I called you,' Medley mumbled. 'You all but rid me down.'

'The men I was guiding had come for their own pur- poses—not mine, not yours. That purpose could only harm us both. I would not for worlds have let them know I have a son.'

'It was as if I'd hailed some stranger!' Medley cried, giving in to his tears. ' 'T'weren't fitting, what you did, sir.'

'Stop snivelling!' his father said, sharp and angry.
'You're not a babe. I say it was for your good. Let that
suffice.'

The knowledge that his father's anger was now added
to the general burden made Medley bold and insolent.
'There's lots must suffice, then. As—how you live with
my mother. You live with her and any'd think you must
be her husband. But now I can see, all on a sudden,
that you're never her husband. You're never her husband
and so you make me a bastard—and so I should go sneaking
about in shame for all of us. That's for my good, is it?'

'Have you come to this of yourself?' his father asked,
quiet now.

'I knew it—I bluv I knew it all my life and never
thought of it—not till you rid by that evening.'

'However long or little, thought of or not thought of,
the end's the same.'

'Yes, surelye—it's the same.'

'I worked the best way for you.'

'And for my mother?' Medley cried bitterly.

'You have not heard her complain.'

'She'm too good!'

'Aye, that's a truth,' Dick Plashet said. 'Too good for
me or any man, God keep her . . . Medley, you know
well that a son inherits from his father—as Simon
Mallory will be master of Mantlemass one day, and Roger
shall have Ghylls Hatch. That's in law. But out of law
there can be no inheritance. Here is the truth—do with
it what you may: I have nothing to bequeath but a name.
I would not for worlds leave any son of mine heir to
that for his fortune.'

'That's riddles,' Medley said, impatient and afraid of
his complete lack of understanding. 'You only talk in
riddles.'

'No man can claim you as my son. No man. Do you hear, even if you do not understand? No man can claim you as my son. In that lies your best future.'

'How can it? How'm I to rejoice in that? What's glad in that? What's good in it—that I must never say I'm your son? You took away my good life, father, that's certain sure. I'll be scorned through all the world!'

'Ah, poor lad,' his father said, smiling a little and very tenderly at this wretched self-pitying cry. 'There's no fault in *you*—so prove it to all the world. The fault is mine, if fault it is. A fault in law. A fault in what we know as virtue. It must bear that. Yes, truly—it is a sin against all we must believe. But it's my sin, my risk—not yours. If I am to be condemned by heaven, Medley, I trust firmly in God it will not be for this.'

He had been standing by the hearth; now he came to sit beside Medley on the bench at the table. He put his arm across the boy's shoulders and said evenly, 'Pray for me. I shall have faith in you for that—and so you must have faith in me. You must believe that what I have done for you is better a thousand times than what the world might do. Pray for me, Medley—that you and I and your dearest mother may live safe together. For if ever it is otherwise, then I must leave you.'

'You must not ever!' Medley cried, turning to his father and clutching at him, feeling himself held strongly as he had not been since babyhood. 'I do surelye trust to you, master. I do indeed—I swear it.' The necessary truth was clear to him—trust for trust, no more questioning or conjecturing and no more blame. This would be what his mother had accepted—nor would he ever be able to ask her if she had solved more riddles, as he suspected, than he could possibly hope to solve as yet. He must accept what mystery there was; he must be content. He wanted with all his heart to do the right thing, but it was bitterly hard. 'I *am* your son . . . ?' he insisted.

'Be sure of that. Why, Medley, if our two faces were taken apart and shuffled—made into a medley—and then re-made, none should tell whose eye was whose!' He gave the boy a last warm pressure and then rose. As he went back towards the hearth to toss a log on the fire and settle it with his toe, he was already retreating into his own world. The flames leapt to show his pale strong face at once sad and resolute.

It was possible that not until two nights ago had Medley understood how much he loved this aloof and dignified man—this 'mysterious father' as Puss Mallory had called him. She had spoken of 'stories with wrong endings'. Perhaps his father's story had a wrong ending and he should not even be here on the forest, living poorly and yet proudly.

'We are agreed, then?' he said, not turning from the fire.

'Yes, sir,' replied Medley, using his careful voice with no *country tricks*, as his father called them. 'Only I wish it were not so.'

'I have wished that. Most, when I was your age or a little more.'

'Because of *your* father . . . ?'

'We are to trust one another, not to question.'

'Yes, sir. I know it.'

'I never knew my father. I'll tell you so much. I only saw him once . . . If any ever speak to you of your grandfather, which is what my whole purpose is intended to avoid, they will offer you his place. When that happens—though I pray it never will—stay firm at home. He died a little more than twenty years past. Nothing he left behind could better you or me. That is most certain . . . Now go and draw the evening's water. Your mother should not be long.'

A week later, Hal Urry came running to Plashet's and said there were to be no more lessons for the old priest had died. He was crying, and it seemed strange, for he had always hated his lessons and was as thick-headed as a bolt of oak. His heart, in his meagre thin body, was made of softer stuff.

'When my hawk die, Melly, he never made no boffle of saying a blessing for it. The new priest, he'll never send no animal to heaven when it die.'

The 'new priest' was Sir Gregory, who had been at the village church for five years and more, but he was from some distant part, Cornwall, they said, or Wales, and he did not understand the foresters nor they him.

'Did he say that?' Medley asked. 'Did he say the hawk should go to heaven?'

'Why else should he bless it? He say it fly nearer heaven than him a'ready . . . I wish I bin a bit deedy in my lessons. He'd a' liked that,' muttered Hal, breaking into sad tears again.

'Does Roger know?'

'Oh, aye—Master Lewis Mallory were with Sir James all night till early morning, till he die. Then he send for Dame Cecily, and she come with Meg and with Peg Bostel, your aunt, and they wash him and lay him out fine. Now there's only to bury him,' said Hal, sniffing hard and wiping the back of his hand across his eyes and nose. 'A'ready I miss him sore,' he said.

'Best go tell Giles, Hal,' said Medley soberly. 'I disremember the time afore I learnt my lessons. Who'll learn us now?'

They stood a moment sadly. Then Hal cheered up and said his father had promised to let him work now. He would be boy at the furnace and run hither and yon as he was told, helping the men and learning how the iron was handled. The furnaces would scarce blow without him, he would be so necessary.

'You'll blow yourself out, sure enough,' said Medley gloomily. The whole world seemed to be changing. He had so much to think about he hardly knew where to start.

When Hal had gone off to the mill to tell the news to Giles Ade, Medley went down to Staglye village. He had never seen a dead man and did not know if he wanted to, but he was sure he needed to make certain Sir James was truly dead by giving him a last greeting. He went across the forest aware that the autumn had moved so swiftly on its way that the end of the year could already be seen—many branches were quite bare, the grass had stopped growing, the fungi had mouldered, the birds were different. The sky was clear now of the last swallow and he wondered, as always, where they hid and spent the winter. Once he had heard his father say that they flew out to sea and plunged below the waves, there to remain until summer came again. But when Medley asked Sir James the old man shrugged and said, 'God knoweth, but I do not,' which was something he said more and more as he grew older and older.

At Staglye there was a crowd of people, both men and women, gathered by the church gate. Sir James had lived and kept his school in the little dwelling at the gate for over ten years after he moved from the palace chapel. Presently the 'new priest' came through the door. He was praying aloud and the crowd mumbled the responses as he passed between them, followed by four men carrying the old man's coffin. He would not be much of a weight, Medley thought, for he had grown as frail as a leaf in the last year or two. Master Mallory followed immediately behind the coffin, being chief mourner, for he had thought much of Sir James, who had been his schoolmaster, as well as his sons'. The coffin was carried into the church and laid before the altar to await burial. Davy's wife, plump Sukey, was beside Medley in the throng, and he heard himself ask her, could they see him, or would the lid be tight?

'Any who wants may see him,' Sukey said. 'Will you take a look at him dead?'

Medley did not answer. He needed to say goodbye. To *look at him dead* was somehow not the same thing at all. He glanced round for help. He saw Dame Cecily leaving the door of the gatehouse, and he pushed his way to her side.

'I never see him since three days, madam,' he said. 'Now there's naun I can tell him for goodbye.'

'Let's wait a little till the rest are gone,' she answered, making no bones about it, understanding his need instantly. She moved aside and Medley went to stand by her. She was very still and contained, a little pale and sad, but serene. For the first time he saw her, not as herself, but as Catherine's mother. 'It was Sir James who married me to my husband, Medley. A long time ago. And after that I recall most how he comforted me when my first baby was born dead. And when the second died of a fever.'

'And when my sister died,' said Medley, 'he came to comfort my mother.'

'But he could also be very merry,' Dame Cecily told him. 'You think only of an old man who taught you your lessons. But I remember him when he delighted in music, and played many instruments for his enjoyment and ours. We shall miss him, Medley.'

'Yes, madam,' agreed Medley. 'We shall miss him sore.'

'Come inside now,' she said, when they had been silent and thinking for a time. 'The rest have gone.'

The church was cold and dim, its thick walls clutching at its thatched roof, holding out the daylight but embracing centuries of prayer and supplication. The coffin was on the chancel steps, covered only with a cloth.

'Will you see him?' Dame Cecily asked. 'Or just stay a moment to pray for his soul?'

'See him,' said Medley, bracing himself.

So she pulled back the cloth. There lay Sir James with pious hands, his white hair combed, his cheeks like marble yet his mouth touched with a familiar smile— half loving and half laughing, as he had so often been to his pupils. He looked both comfortable and content, a very old man who would have little difficulty in making a place for himself, whatever world he happened to be in.

'There,' said Dame Cecily. 'Now, Medley, there is no need for tears—you can see that.'

'Yes, madam,' he said again, but very tight in his throat. He watched her pull the cloth back into place, rather as if she were tucking up an invalid for the night. She knelt a moment, so he knelt, too, and then they went out into the daylight together.

'There's Master Mallory with the horses,' she said, 'wondering what I'm about. Good-day, Medley. Tell your mother that the salve worked wonders. My daughter will have no scar from the burns. Thank her for me.'

'Yes, madam,' he said, for the third time at least. He watched her walk across to her husband. Master Mallory turned from talk to smile at her. He held her horse while she mounted—jossed-up, as Medley would say—then turned to his own mount. They rode away side by side, soberly because of the occasion, but Dame Cecily found time to turn and smile at Medley, and nod as it were to encourage him.

Medley went home by a roundabout way because he needed to consider. The sky was now overcast and the wind that blew sneakingly over the forest was a winter wind. Before he came to Plashet's he saw his mother outside the house looking for him, and he waved and began to run. The moment she saw him, Anis ran too, hurrying down the track and meeting him by the stream.

'Medley,' she cried at once, 'you saw the strangers your father guided last week or so. What kind of men were they? How did they look? Now tell me if you can, for I'm sore frit, Melly.'

'Why frit, mother? They'm gone long ago. Lunnon sorts, I'd say—like Master Crespin that came visiting!'

'How many, then?'

'Three.'

'Did your father tell you any tales of them later?'

'That warn't what my father tell me. That were summat quite else.' He frowned at her, for she was trembling and her hands could not be still, but clenched together or picked at her apron.

'I think they come again this day,' she said.

'And if they did—what then?' But he felt a creeping unease himself, partly because of her manner, partly because of what this talk of the strangers recalled. They had come for their own purposes, his father had said. He had not wanted them to know he had a son—well, all that followed came from that. 'Did you see the strangers, then, mother?' he asked.

'I saw them. I saw them coming along the ghyll, and I called to your father. "There's some come for guiding,"

I said—for I saw they must have rid by Goodales, and
I thought they'd a' been sent on.'

'Well, then? What happened then?'

'Your father come to where I were by the window.
He stood at my shoulder and look out. He—he put his
hand on my arm—but he were going, even then—'

'Going?'

'From the room. From the house. From you and me.
I turned quick and I caught his hand and held on. But
it might have been the devil was tugging him away. I
lost him. At the last he went so quick I stumbled. I run
out, Melly, seeking him. I saw the way he went—there
were a bough swinging and the old horse went galloping
up the field. He must've give a whistle, and the old horse
heard, for he took the gate like a two-year-old. And that's
the last I see of either.'

Anis seemed to sway a little as she remembered, and
Medley put his arm round her and held her. He had
grown in the last weeks. He was certainly the taller now.

'Go on, mother.'

'Then, when I'd run back in home, there come the
three strangers to the door. And ask for him.'

'To guide them?'

'They didn't say that.'

'What, then?'

'They say: "We come for Richard."' Anis looked
sharply at Medley and paused a second. ' "Who's that?"
I asked. And one said, "Your husband." So I said, "No." '
Anis thrust away from Medley and seemed to steady
herself. 'Well, that were true at the least,' she muttered.
'Then one say, "Where does Richard live? Where shall
we find him?" "How can I tell?" says I. "I've no notion
where—why should I have?" And that were true, too.'

'They only needed a guide,' Medley said, hoping to

convince himself, but already sure it was nothing so simple as that. 'What else?'

'How can I say what else? I only know there was a lot strange and secret happened to your father afore ever he come this way to the forest. He hid from something. What he hid from was nothing bad—I see that in all I know of him. So put that out of your mind.'

'T'id'n in my mind.'

'In your eyes it is,' she said.

'No,' he said. 'Come home now, mother, and sit by the fire. There's naun we can do but wait till he get back.'

His mother looked at him so deeply that his bones seemed to shiver.

'He won't niver get back,' she said.

6
Winter and Rough Weather

After a week or two Medley knew for certain what his
mother had recognised immediately: his father would not
return.

'The neighbours need not know it,' Anis said.

'They'd better, mother. Likely we'll need their help.'

'No, Medley! You and me—we'll do well enough. I
won't have it known—now that's for certain, so don't
you get nabbling.'

'Where'd he go? How'll he live?'

'There's always work for a man that knows how.'

'Oh, mother, we'll miss him sore,' cried Medley;
and watched her turn away sharply, for she would not

show him her distress. 'Oh, why should he leave us, mother?'

'He were druv to it by the past,' she muttered. 'Now, Melly, I'll say one thing, and niver again. You know well b'now that your father never took me to church. Not that he were wed already—that I do know and believe truly. No—it were some other thing, long back, that he feared might come again.'

'And did come again, mother . . .'

'Aye.' Anis straightened her shoulders. 'A blessing, howsomever, that we had so many years together . . . You'm halfway to a man's strength, Medley—more'n halfway. We'll do well enough so long's Master Mallory let us keep the cottage. And I know certainly he never would do other.'

Apart from his guiding, Dick Plashet had often gone to far corners of the village and beyond when special building skills were called for—he knew tricks of masonry and joinery far beyond any forester. Therefore his absence was not remarked for some time. Though he was a tenant of Mantlemass, what he did over and above his service to the lord of the manor was his own concern and always had been. Anis did more than he for Mantlemass, and her cordials and salves, her medicines and preserves had come to be accepted as the tithe due from Plashet's.

That first winter after his father left home was a hard one for Medley and Anis. The summer had been long and fine and the winter set in fiercely from the very first day that the wind swung into the north. North by north-east it blew for weeks on end, snow threatening but never falling, the ground drying and bleaching as Medley himself grew and toughened with every day. He set at once about the business of keeping himself and his mother, and in the last of October and through

November they worked incessantly to get in provender enough to see them through till the spring. The logs to be hewn now must be man-size. There was no one but Medley to find rabbits for meat, to dig the hard ground clear of this year's rootcrop and prepare the neighbouring strip for the spring. They had a third larger strip, which had been planted in two parts, one barley and one oats. They had a good harvest off this piece, and took a fair lot of grain to the mill. Giles, who had been Medley's schoolfellow, worked now for his father, Miller Ade.

'Where's Dick Plashet, then?' the miller asked. 'He bring his own grain most years.'

'He's off building a gentleman's house,' lied Medley. 'I'm gaffer now!'

The miller and his son laughed at this, and as usual the trip to the mill was as merry as a holiday. John Ade was a big fair man, kind to his children of both sorts, but soft as butter with the girls among them.

'Giles, put the sack on the donkey and drive it down to Plashet's,' he said when the meal was ready.

'Thankee, Master Ade,' said Medley, for the thought of humping the sack home had worried him. He and Giles went off across the forest together. But though they had behaved like children together only a few months ago, now both were changed. Giles's cheeks and chin were fluffy with the beginnings of a beard, and his voice was in his boots. He talked about girls in a rather leering way. Then he said something that made Medley chill.

'Likely I'll come to your mother for a love charm, if Jane Urry don't fancy me at first.'

'She can't give you what she don't have to sell.'

'Goo on, you,' said Giles, butting his elbow into Medley's ribs. 'Any know she's a wise woman.'

'Come for a charm, you'll get a purge!' cried Medley
in a rage that was mostly fear.

At this Giles turned an unpleasant red. He checked
the donkey, tipped off the sack of meal, turned away and
went off up the hill in silence. With great difficulty, his
mind full of unease, Medley somehow dragged the sack
the rest of the way home.

It was good to have the flour stored. Besides, there
were apples on hay in the cellar, a sack of hazel nuts and
another of chestnuts from the one sweet chestnut tree
standing on what was said to be the boundary of the
old lost palace ground; a number of seedlings had sprung
up, but none was big enough yet to bear fruit. Medley
and Anis had ten or twelve pounds of honey for themselves from their own hives, for honey was used in many
of Anis's concoctions and they had always to restrict
themselves. Besides all this, there was a hog that had been
ready for killing at the very time Dick Plashet went
away. Medley had been forced to deal with that himself,
and had botched the job, and wept over it. However, he
had contrived to skin and cut up the carcase, and then
got salt enough for curing. Tom Bostel had given them
some, for he always helped Anis when he could, though
secretly, because of Peg. Rufus Goodale had supplied
the rest, payment in kind for Dick's services as a guide;
he asked after Dick, but did not press the matter, though
Medley knew as he walked away that Rufus watched
him go and scratched his chin as if he wondered what
was afoot. So now the pig's haunches hung curing above
the fire, the rest was in tubs in the cellar. They got a
good bladder of lard from the creature, though it had
cared for itself about the forest and had little chance of
getting the careful fattening they gave the pigs at Mantlemass. Lard, too, was used by Anis in many salves and

ointments. They had not managed to get many hops, so it would be very small beer for the two of them in the days to come. But there were plenty of herbs for brewing other drinks that Anis said were healthy. The herbs hung in bunches among the kitchen rafters—parsley, mint of more than one sort, fennel and marjoram and lemon balsam, thyme and sage, tansy and chamomile—and a handful of a plant Dame Cecily grew, which must have come from another land—Sir James had found the seed in an old earthenware crock when he was still at the palace chapel; it might have been used in the palace kitchens, he thought. No one had ever found out what it was called.

There was no snow until the second week in December, but after that it continued off and on right round to the first of March. In all that time there was no complete thaw and for weeks on end it was not possible to move about the forest at all. It was now that Medley remembered his father's books, hidden in their dry safe place. He took them out and unwrapped them from the sheepskin bag that contained them, and spread them over the table.

'Now what will you do?' asked Anis.

'My father had me taught. I'll not forget what I learned all those years.'

'He set great store by they books, Melly. I do sometimes think they could bring him back—'

'But not you nor me?' Medley asked. 'That's not how you mostly speak of him.'

'Nor as I recall him, neither. Perhaps I just hoped the books might bring him back.' Anis smiled slightly. 'Take care you don't spoil 'em.'

'Why would I? But have books and not read 'em—well, that's like having gold and spending naught.'

There were six books in all. One was a great volume weighing almost as much as the sack of meal Giles Ade had tipped off the donkey's back. It was written on thick velvety skin with rough edges, and the margins were decorated in gold and colour. All the psalms were written there, and at the head of each page the first letter was adorned and twined about with flowers. The second book was much smaller, and less grand, and this contained nothing but poems in Latin; on the first page was the poet's name: Horace. This book was much worn. The leather down the back was darkly stained where it had been held in the hand of the reader. There were some pages so tattered they almost fell out when the book was opened.

Next came a flat, thin book, the covers tied with leather thongs, and in it there were charts and maps of distant places, oceans with ships and dolphins; and a map, too, of the heavens, with all the stars. Then also there was a little herbal, which had been useful to Anis—indeed her skills had been built on what the book contained, and it had been read so often at her request that now she knew it almost all by heart. The fifth was a Holy Missal, with all the feasts of the church and their ceremonies; and last was a book with half its pages empty, and in this Medley had seen his father writing from time to time. This book he set aside and never opened, for it seemed too private to be read.

Of the rest, he read every page. The snow was at the window and the light was sharp. Medley blessed the window, that his father had made with small pieces of glass that Sir James had gathered up out of the ruins of the palace chapel. For some time there had been glass but no lead in which to set it. Then a charcoal burner came to trade for a pitcher of milk, and the price was a

length of lead guttering he had stolen long ago from the
ruins up on the high bank above the river. So the lead
was melted and used to hold the glass and the window
was glazed at last. Its little panes set a pattern on the
table when the sun shone through. As Medley stooped
intently over his father's books in the bitter winter, the
pages were tinted white or green or gold, or they were
shadowed by the one pane that retained some painting
from its chapel days—the eyes and nose, but no more,
of some nameless saint.

Throughout almost all this winter Plashet's was cut off
from Mantlemass, from the village and from the road
that led south past the mill to the market town. Even
when there was a slight thaw, this deeper part of the
forest held its drifts and banks. Medley and Anis went
to bed at dusk and rose with the first cold light. They
could not be prodigal with wood to make the fire leap
so that they could see by it. They had gathered rushes
enough but only a small amount of mutton fat for dipping
them. Medley lay on his bed by the hearth, but the
fire damped down with peat could not warm him, and
he shivered as he slept. The hens roosted among the
rafters and the cat crept to Medley's side and he took
her under the thin covers for his own comfort as well as
hers. In the one room above, that Dick Plashet had built
with Master Mallory's permission, Medley heard his
mother cry out in her sleep, and often enough he heard
her weeping—she wept for love and loneliness, more
than he could hope to understand. Medley, too, lay
thinking of the man who had gone away, wondering if
any ill had come to him, or if he was settling himself to
a new life—as most certainly he had done at least once
before.

On the first day in the New Year that the tracks became

passable, the lord of the manor of Mantlemass, Master Lewis Mallory, rode up to the door of Plashet's. Medley was milking the cow in her stall when he heard the horse thudding up the path from the river. His heart almost stopped beating and his hands were still—for a second he thought that his father had come back. Then he heard Master Mallory call out to Anis. As he stripped the last of the thin winter milk and set the pail aside, Medley knew that life was about to begin again, that the outside world still existed, that he had a friend called Roger, whose sister had come to seem like a star once seen then lost among clouds. He went out of doors feeling as if a long dream was over.

Anis was standing by Master Lewis's horse, looking up at the rider, who was muffled against the cold and wore his red cap like a woodpecker's, that had given him the nickname hereabouts of *Yaffle*. Anis saw Medley and called to him, 'Master Lewis is asking for your father.' She sounded very strained and nervous.

'My father's from home, sir,' said Medley. He was surprised to hear how firm and deep his voice sounded.

'Then he's been from home all winter-long,' said Lewis Mallory, 'for he could not travel till three days ago. Even today the horse moves warily, and the dogs stayed behind for all the whistling I could raise up.'

He was smiling, but in a rather puzzled way, and this increased as neither Medley nor Anis answered. He began to frown. He looked powerful and fine, Medley thought, sitting his horse in the pale sunshine as if they had almost grown together. He was not handsome but his face was strong and open and content—a face, Anis had once said, that offered a greeting.

'Well, then?' he said, a trifle impatient. 'Is it so?'

'Aye, sir,' said Medley. 'All winter.' He knew the truth

had to come out, and better now, and to Master Lewis, than later to some already inquisitive neighbour.

'Then you have been hard pressed, I fear. Why did you not send the boy with word of this, Anis? There were days, surely, when he could have got through?'

'At first I was not sure,' mumbled Anis, turning red at the lie.

'Your father will be sad to hear this. He has worried about you through the winter in any event.' He looked keenly from Medley to his mother. 'Where *is* Dick Plashet, Anis? What is he about?'

Anis hesitated. Then she said reluctantly, 'There's no answer to that, master. He go one day and never come back.'

'Then he must be searched for. I shall see to it.'

'No.'

'But some ill or accident may have overtaken him.'

'No,' said Anis. This time she looked up and her voice and her eyes were steady. 'He'll not come again,' she said. 'He'm gone as he always might.'

'Well, truly—he always was a strange man. But I never would have thought to find he's left you and Medley.'

'He had his reasons,' said Anis.

'Well,' he seemed at a loss. 'I must think of this. I am riding round to see how the tenants fare after the long winter. This is my first call and I am given bad tidings.'

'I am sorry for it,' Anis said. For the first time there was a break in her voice and she looked at her hands instead of at his face.

'I've come also to learn what cordials and so on you can give us, Anis,' he said, as if to distract her. 'The winter has consumed our supplies. Have you something I can take in my saddle bags?'

'Aye, indeed,' she said, and almost ran indoors.

Lewis Mallory frowned down at Medley. 'This news disturbs me very much indeed. Is your mother right? Shall your father truly not return, think you?'

Standing in the chill bright morning with the melting snow gurgling away into the myriad forest streams, Medley admitted finally that his mother was right.

'I bluv—' he began, then corrected himself—'I believe, sir, he may not.' Then the horror of what he had admitted struck him so hard that his mouth opened as if he would cry out. He knew how he must look by the expression of concern on Master Mallory's face.

'God help you, Medley, boy,' he said. 'This is a cruel blow your father has dealt you.' He bent out of the saddle and touched Medley's shoulder. 'You must take heart. You have friends and I'll see to it that you're cared for. Surelye,' he cried, as rough and strong as any in the forest, 'it don't bear reckoning, how hard a thing he done. But you'm a bright suent lad, Medley Plashet, as can rise above a bannicking, I bluv. You'm come to years enough.'

This made Medley grin widely for all his wretchedness, for Lewis Mallory sounded and looked like Roger in the same mood. And as if the thought of Roger was plain to read in Medley's face, Roger's father gathered up his reins, and said, 'Bring the cordials and things yourself. The track's pretty stoachy, but you can manage. Your grandfather will be glad to see you—and so will my son.'

Then he wheeled away instantly and was gone, so that Anis ran out of the door in astonishment and concern.

'Where'd he go? What happen?'

'He say I should take the things myself.'

Medley was still smiling. The winter was over, the snow was vanishing away. He was too young to think, as his mother thought, that both were bound to come again.

7
The Wise Woman

That spring Peg Bostel came to her sister's house of her own free will. Anis was throwing out corn for the hens, and Medley was standing near talking to her about the cow. They were absorbed in their own affairs and certainly not expecting visitors. Not that unexpected callers were rare. Now that Anis was on her own with Medley, she was called more and more often to give advice in cases of sickness.

'She'm rarely old, mother,' Medley said of the cow. 'The milk's very little. I wonder should she be slaughtered now.' He spoke roughly, for he was at once anxious to appear tough and manly, and deeply sad to think the little cow's days were numbered. How often in the dark mornings, fumbling with stiff cold hands to milk her, he had warmed himself against her flank and seen her turn her head kindly towards him. 'She done well for us these years,' he said.

Anis threw out the last grain to the scurrying hens and sighed. 'Where'll we ever get another cow?'

'That's a mystery,' Medley agreed. 'But we might make do with a goat. Less to feed, and old Deb Goodale say she'd let us have a nanny and a kid.'

'Better not. Not from Deb.'

'Why not? She's not pretty or young,' grinned Medley, 'but her heart's kind.'

'I know. But I want no gifts from Deb, poor soul!'

'She'd be glad. For my father's sake, so she tell me.'

'There's plenty ready to call Deb a witch, Melly.'

'It's her beard, mother!'

'Plenty to name me, too,' Anis said quietly. 'To tell truth.'

'Why—you got no beard, mother!'

'Laugh, then. I say it's best not to trade wi' Deb Goodale.'

'Whoever name you,' said Medley, 'hammers his own coffin. Where'd they be, making do wi'out your medicines and such?'

'Well,' said Anis, 'folks don't think much before they act.'

'We'll get another cow, then. Or a goat from somewheres other.'

The winter had hardened Medley. He had grown a lot and broadened, too, in spite of the meagre meals he and Anis had to make do with. And because he had read so much, and told his mother of all he had read, his mind had stretched along with his bones and his muscles. Not

quite six months after his father's going, he knew himself
to be almost a different person. No longer a schoolboy,
that was sure—almost a scholar, instead. The toughness
of the life he saw ahead was no longer a matter of dread,
but of challenge. He did indeed still yearn after his
father, and puzzle over all the remaining riddles; but
he accepted that there was nothing he could do to solve
them at this time. One day they would be solved. One
day he would see his father again, and being no longer
a child, demand to know.

It was easier for Medley than for his mother. He looked
at her keenly often enough, as he looked at her now.
Her face remained shadowed by her grief and by her
loneliness. But she was a young and energetic woman.
It came to Medley then that if any man wooed her there
was no lawful reason why she should not accept him as
a husband. But he thought, because of how she had lived
unwed with Dick Plashet, and such things were never
secret, men might expect easier favours.

He had not considered this before and it shook him.
He almost spoke—and then saw a woman crossing the
river by the stepping stones. It was his aunt Peg Bostel.

'Well, look . . .' he said, and grinned.

Anis, however, ran forward crying, 'What's amiss?
Peg! Is it father?'

'Father's well enough,' said Peg. 'It's you I come
to see.'

'Come indoors, and welcome!' Anis cried. She smiled
at her sister, but Peg looked black as ever. She picked
her way up the path that Medley had mended since
winter, digging out loads of old furnace slag for the job.

'Here's your aunt Peg come visiting, Melly,' his mother
said. He heard the gladness in her voice and knew that
she had instantly forgiven Peg every slight and slur.

'I see that boy often enough about Mantlemass,' Peg
Bostel said. 'It's you I've come to talk to, sister.'

'Come in,' Anis said again. 'I'm glad you're come, Peg.
I am indeed.'

They went together into the house, and Peg shoved
the door closed. Medley was left to his own concerns.
He saw that the woodstack was getting low, but there
were three-foot lengths left by his father standing against
the wall, so he fetched one and set about splitting and
cutting it. As he worked he found so much in his mind
he began to sing and whistle to stop himself thinking.
Straightening himself after dealing with one bolt, he saw
two women passing on the far bank. The forest was
becoming busier as the season advanced. The women
were looking towards Plashet's and whispering. He knew
one of them, for she was wife to the smith in the village.
The younger he thought must be her son's wife, that he
had married at midsummer. Medley saw that she was
already carrying her first child, and might perhaps ask
advice and help from his mother. So he waved and called
out to them.

The younger woman opened her mouth to reply, but
the older shushed her sharply and drew her on, an arm
almost protectively around her. As she hurried her
daughter-in-law along, the smith's wife looked back over
her shoulder. Her expression was pinched and unkind
and, as if that were not enough, she crossed herself, very
broadly and ostentatiously.

Medley swung the axe, but then set it down, for he
found that he was shaking and cold and all the force had
gone out of him. The fact that Anis herself knew how
vulnerable she might be, and had spoken of it so recently,
together with his own thoughts about her husbandless
state, made up such a mountain of worry in Medley's

mind that for a moment he felt there was nothing for it but flight. Before some terrible evil overtook them, they must leave Plashet's and live elsewhere, in some new place where no one knew them except as a widow and her son. If they might only seek out his father! But he knew they must not, for there the danger was unnamed—he trusted his father still, believing implicitly that what he had done he had done for their sake rather than his own. It must be a grave danger indeed that he had hoped to avert, for he could not have been ignorant of what perils might be left behind.

The door flung open as Medley stood trying to accept and absorb his fears. Peg Bostel flounced out and strode off down the path without a word or a look in his direction. He could see she was in a state of black anger. She was almost running by the time she had crossed back over the stepping stones, and within seconds she had disappeared. Anis stood in the doorway and watched her go.

'What she say, mother? What she want?'

'She ask for a philtre,' Anis said. Her lip curled. 'A love philtre, God save us! At her age! And who she aims at, Melly, I hardly dare name. None but Rufus Goodale!'

'Older than grandfather!' Medley cried.

'One more such winter and I'll be too old even for him, she say. Lord,' muttered Anis, 'I'd not wish Peg on poor Rufus. I respect his kind heart.'

'You send her off, then?'

'Aye.' Anis shook her head and clenched her hands together. 'A pretty pass, when my own sister ask such things of me. And I thought she come here today to make up all quarrels. Well—that's done with. She'll not come calling again, I reckon.'

7

Medley said nothing. He was afraid his mother might be wrong, and that Peg would come again, though not in friendship. Or that she might see to it that others came.

Roger and Catherine rode up to Plashet's a month or more later, needing Medley to give a hand with driving sheep. They were to go to pasture five or six miles away to the south-west, where the manor of Mantlemass claimed other lands. Roger was leading a third horse for Medley. He had bread and meat enough for all of them, he said, stowed in his saddle bag.

Medley had work enough to do at home, but this was not only a longed-for holiday, it was service to his lord and—happily—was not to be avoided. He mounted joyfully, shouted goodbye to Anis, and rode off with the others to fetch the sheep, waiting with two drovers, who must trudge afoot, and the shepherd who would remain with the flock. There were four dogs fussing among the sheep and longing to be off.

Catherine was wearing a russet red cloak with the hood thrown back and she rode unusually sedately.

'This time a year ago you strid your horse like a lad,' Medley reminded her.

'I'm grown,' she said. 'I am to try to be a lady, my mother says.'

'Shall it go hard, Puss?'

'It shall go very hard, Melly,' said Catherine, scowling. 'So hard I doubt I'll bear it.'

'Call 'em up, then, Dan!' Roger shouted to one of the drovers. 'Get 'em moving, now.'

The drovers and the shepherd called to the dogs, the dogs ran barking, the sheep rushed hither and yon, wildly baa-ing, the lambs at their tails bleating and crying.

There was a great rolling April sky, full of hoddern grey and purple, with bright white clouds. They would be lucky if they escaped a drenching. The spring had been as gentle as the winter had been fierce, and the sheep were moving to lush and gracious living; next time they were driven it would be plumply to market. The progress was leisurely, for the lambs were young and must not be hustled. The shepherd was the one who called a halt every mile, and the lambs rushed round their mothers. The flock seemed to heave into waves of wool as the lambs' tails wagged to and fro and they butted furiously into the ewes, so that there came the long rhythmic movement over the whole huge flock.

The three friends rode leisurely, most often finding excuse to stay together, though they did occasionally justify their presence there by riding along the outskirts of the flock and keeping the animals in bounds. And at each halt they rested together, glad of the chance to talk, for although the winter was now so long over, there had been too much work for all of them to give much opportunity for meeting.

'Simon goes to London a week from now,' Roger told Medley.

'Why, what to do, then?' cried Medley. 'What shall Simon do in London?'

'Learn to be a gentleman,' said Catherine, 'just as I must be a lady.'

'He goes to my mother's cousins,' Roger explained. 'It is Lord Digby's household and they are about the court, she says.'

'Lord save us all,' said Medley, amazed, for he thought of Simon as a countryman. 'How shall he return?'

'With scented hair and some twort faddy Lunnon lass to wife, shouldn't wonder,' cried Roger. 'That'll larn our Puss here to be meek. There's no girl can stomach her sister-in-law, so old Meg tell me.'

'One thing's certain sure,' snapped Catherine. 'Simon never will speak so broad as you're doing now, brother Roger—never again, he won't. And his faddy wife, she'll mince and mangle so none shall understand a word she say!'

'And another thing that's certain sure,' Roger said, 'is that the same shall happen to you, Mistress Kitten, when the time comes and they send you away to our cousins or some other grand household.'

Catherine was riding between the boys, and they were walking the horses, but this made her pull up short and sit very still, so they checked, too.

'That'll never be,' she said.

'Why should it?' asked Medley, and his heart seemed to jump up against his throat, so that he gasped slightly.

'Why, for the same reason that Simon is sent, chucklehead. That gentry act so for their sons and daughters. And Mallorys, God help 'em, are gentry folk. Though I think our parents would sooner forget this part of their duty, I do indeed.'

'I'll run away,' said Catherine fiercely, 'but I'll never go to London.'

'You'll stay unwed all your life, if you don't. Who's to come courting here in the forest? Run away or sent away, you'll still be from home—so as well be comfortable. Though they do say,' he told her, grinning, 'that our cousin Digby's wife, the Lady Susannah, keeps a fine sharp tongue in her head!'

'Who say, brother?'

'I had it of old Nick Forge—he's often there on business of our mother's.'

'Shall you be sent, too?' Medley asked Roger, feeling his whole life changing with every word.

'I doubt that. One, I'm but the second son and need not be so fine. Two, my heritage is horses and Ghylls Hatch, and none else I'd ask for. And three—well, maybe in the end I'll turn out neither lord nor lackey but something other.' He looked about him and saw the flock straggling. 'Kick up your pony, Kitten. The sheep must be druv and we're doing little enough.'

Catherine kicked up her horse to such effect that she galloped off and left them all, riding on alone, the task in hand forgotten, and anger in every line and movement of her.

Roger glanced at Medley and frowned a little at what he saw in his face. It was an anxious, not an angry frown. 'Nothing goes easy once we get grown out of childish times,' he said. 'It's these midway years I hate—treated like a boy and expected to behave like a man! It's hard.' He was silent a moment, riding neck and neck with Medley, the sheep still forgotten. It was some time since they had had a chance to speak to one another privately, and much had happened to both of them in the way of growing up during the past months. 'Have you any word of your father?' Roger asked, after opening his mouth more than once and then closing it again.

'None.'

'If I say what I must, Melly, shall we still be friends?'

Medley did not turn his head, but said, 'Yes. If you say it's what you must say.'

'There's talk about the forest.'

'About my father?'

'Somewhat. But he's away, so he won't answer.'

Again there moved in Medley's mind that mountain of unease that seemed to press upon his thoughts. 'You mean my mother, then.' He glanced at Roger and saw him looking distressed and uncertain—which seemed strange, seeing who he was, and older by two years than Medley. 'Well—now you begun, best tell all.'

'Seeing she's so wise with herbs and brews,' Roger said, 'she'd be better not keeping the cat indoors.'

'It's a pretty cat,' replied Medley, purposely obtuse.

'Be fair with me, Melly; I'm not mocking, so don't you, neither. One thing go on to another with country folk. Davy told me as solemn as solemn that his Sue heard your mother talking to the cow—and the cow answering plain for all to hear!'

Medley gave a hoot of laughter that startled his horse. 'What they argyfy about?'

'I said I'm not mocking. Every wise woman's a witch to some.'

'There's plenty could've died wi'out her. You know that.'

'They know it, too. But there's one or two couldn't ever have been cured—like the charcoal burner's baby. Your mother tended the baby, and did her best, no doubt, but she's alone now and so they got talking. You know what I'm saying. My father says you should come to Mantlemass and live with your grandfather.'

'Not while my aunt Peg Bostel's home—mother never would do that.'

'Why, Peg's to marry old Rufus—don't you know of it, then? Next week, I take it to be. That's common gossip. I wonder your grandfather never spoke of it last time you saw him.'

'He'd be ashamed of her, I'd think—Rufus is as old as grandfather. And what'll he do when she goes?'

'That's answered soon as asked, Medley. Your mother shall care for him.'

'And did your father truly say so?' Medley asked.

'He and my mother, too.'

'Well, I do thank them for their kind care, Roger. And you for an honest friend. But I shall see my mother come to no harm.'

'Don't be too much from home,' Roger said.

There was a warning so horrifying in Roger's quiet words that Medley cried, 'I'm from home now!'

'You cannot be at her side forever. There's the worst trouble. Don't look so, Melly. I only meant—take care. Come on. A mile more and we'll have the sheep stowed. I'll ride home with you and see that all's well. But think of what my father says.'

By the time they reached the grassland, each drover carried a lamb under either arm, and the shepherd had bundled up three. Both Roger and Medley had been pressed into service and carried a couple each on the saddle, while the ewes ran behind. The shepherd kept on grumbling and saying they'd been moved too young, and there'd be losses, and who'd be blamed but him? But he said this every year.

Catherine was waiting when the boys rode up. She was peering in at the door of the shepherd's stone hovel, and pinched her nose and grimaced as they joined her. Roger and the drovers saw the sheep safe, and the shepherd took over his charge. Then the young Mallorys and Medley turned their horses' heads and made for home. Catherine complained that she was hungry, and what of the food in the saddle bags? Roger said she must wait. Medley had to get home.

'Must I starve?' Catherine demanded. 'Shall you let Melly Plashet be our master?'

Roger did not answer, but put his horse to a gallop up a long ride over hilly country. Catherine hung behind obstinately, and Medley waited for her, because he was bound by love and courtesy as no brother could be.

'Please,' he urged her. 'I'm fussed that my mother's alone.'

Catherine's expression changed immediately and he knew that she, too, had spoken of this matter. She urged her horse, then, and was away, with Medley on her heels. It was a good gallop on a good day, the rain still holding off, but the only joy in it for Medley was the sight of Catherine ahead, and how she turned back to look for him. And he remembered turning back after shouting goodbye to his mother that morning, but not pausing long enough to hear her make any objection to his going just then. She could not have done, he told himself, because of his duty to Lewis Mallory, yet he felt now that she might have tried to prevent him. This day was the same as any other day and on any day disaster could strike. By the time he was a mile from home he had convinced himself that his mother would have tried to keep him at home because she had some inner warning of trouble . . .

Now the urge to reach home was so intense that Medley spurred his horse to overtake first Catherine and then Roger, and he pounded on with the turf flying under the horse's hooves and the wind whistling past his face. Approaching from this direction he came to Plashet's from the woodland, breaking out of the trees and looking down on the thatch and the plume of smoke from the chimney his father had made.

There was no surprise whatsoever in the sight of a small knot of people, two or three women, four or five lads, moving slowly up the path from the river. He was still too far away to hear voices, but he picked out the smith's wife, and her sister, who was married to the miller, and was Giles Ade's mother. Giles was there, too. It was when he saw Giles and remembered their last meeting that the final drop of blood seemed to drain out of Medley's veins, leaving him weak and trembling.

Then he saw his mother come to the door and stand on the step looking towards the crowd.

Medley tried to shout to her—to go inside and bar the door—but he had no voice and he was too far away, anyway. Anis must have known what she should do, for she took a step backwards, but at that moment the little cat streaked up the path ahead of the strangers, and tucked in behind her skirts. Someone shouted out, then, and the sound released Medley and sent his horse scrambling and slipping down the hillside. He saw one of the lads stoop, and then a stone hurtled towards the cottage. The cat scuttled from shelter and sprang on the roof. The second stone went straight to its mark. Struck full between the eyes, the cat rolled down the roof and dropped at Anis's feet.

Roger had caught Medley up and was plunging down the hill immediately behind him. Anis stooped over the dead cat. She looked up as Medley reached the door and swung out of the saddle.

'Get inside, mother!'

At the sight of him the crowd turned instantly and began to jostle back down the path to the river. Only Giles Ade stood his ground. He still had a stone in his hand, and he swung his arm, turning back his sleeve as he did so.

Medley had Anis by the arm and was pushing her inside when Giles shouted out:

'Medley! Medley Plashet! There's for you!'

Medley turned instinctively, then ducked as he saw the stone fly. This third stone caught Anis as the second had caught the cat, and just as quietly, just as finally, she fell.

Roger said, 'She's died, Melly,' and almost choked on the words.

'She look that way another time, Roger. A bough fell on her in the forest. She looked then like she were dead. But she woke.'

Roger put his arm round Medley and said again, 'She's died. She won't wake this time.'

Catherine was standing with her hands pressed to her mouth, looking down at Anis. When Roger said this she came to life and threw her arms round Medley in her turn and broke into tears.

'Don't you, now,' he said. He put his cheek against her hair as she clasped him tight, then pulled her hands away because he thought Roger might not care to see his sister so free, but would not want to rebuke her at this moment. He thought of this, perhaps, to delay the other thoughts that would have to be admitted. And just as he had seemed to feel his life's blood going out of him as he looked down at Plashet's and knew he could not prevent what was going to happen, so now he felt as if he brimmed over with despair. If he had not moved when Giles called out, would the stone have hit him, as intended, and perhaps quite harmlessly? He would never know this, never.

'I'll fetch my father,' Roger said. He was in the saddle before he called to his sister, 'Come home!'

'I'll stay.'

Roger hesitated a second only; then he rode off fast.

'It is true she'm dead?' Medley asked Catherine.

'Yes,' she said. She looked at Medley as she had looked at him when she saw his tattered shirt that day last year when she dropped the lamp and was burnt. Then she knelt down beside Anis and without any fear took her hands and laid them on her breast, so that she looked comfortable and meek—but not herself any more, for she had never been meek. Catherine put her own hands briefly over Anis's eyes, and stooped right down and kissed her cheek, as if it belonged to her own living mother. 'Should we not cover her?' she asked. 'I think she should be covered.'

Medley looked about him for a second, as if he expected to recognise his mother somewhere in the air about him. Then he went indoors without speaking. The inside of the cottage was like a great cold well to him. He went up the ladder into the little chamber she had shared with his father, and in which she had stayed solitary since he went away. On the bed was that coverlet of 'tawny-medley' he had been wrapped in, so his father had often told him, when he was born. He took it up and carried it outside. It was faded and tattered by now, but he wrapped it round his mother and then took her in his arms as he crouched on the ground, thinking she should be carried inside. He was still holding her in a helpless fashion, not knowing how fast and bitter the tears ran down his face, when Roger returned with his father. So it was Master Lewis Mallory who carried poor Anis into her home and laid her on the settle.

'God rest her soul,' he said softly. 'She was full of courage . . . Ride for Sir Gregory, Roger. Catherine, my child, off home now and tell your mother and Tom Bostel what has happened.'

'Oh, father, be kind to poor Melly Plashet!' Catherine cried, weeping.

'He shall be cared for. Never fear.' Master Lewis smiled at his daughter and watched her go out to her horse. 'Now, Medley,' he said, when she had gone, 'you must come to Mantlemass. I'll no more leave you to the forest than I'd leave my own. Whoever did this shall be punished.'

'I misremember who threw the stone,' Medley mumbled. 'What good to punish once she's dead? That can't bring her back. If my father were here . . .' His tears choked him and he stood trying to stop them.

'He never should have left you.'

'I say he had reason,' Medley got out. 'I'd like to find out what it could be—sometime before I die.'

He stood by the hearth in the small room that had once seemed warm and full of life, and nothing was left to him of that time. Then he remembered that his father's books were safe in their hiding place. He felt it necessary to fetch them, and to spread them on the table while Master Lewis watched, that both of them might be reminded of what was slipping away so fast it seemed already as if it had never happened. Medley looked around him, aware that he had failed to stop his tears and smearing his hands angrily over his face. He was nothing, he was nobody, he had nothing, not even a true name . . . As he thought this it was as if he echoed something that had gone before, that he could not in fact know about. Perhaps his father had had such thoughts—perhaps it was just so that he had been left, and that was why he had made a life that was openly alien to him. That life had run, if not easily, in modest content—until the day three strangers whom Medley had never heard named, appeared about the forest; and everything was changed.

There was the sound of horses outside, as Roger returned with the priest.

'I wish it were Sir James,' said Medley, and again his grief choked him, adding to its sum the loss of the old man.

'Sir Gregory is a greater man than you know,' Lewis Mallory said. 'Give him a decent greeting. He will take this matter very sore. Let him help you.'

So Medley went to the door, however reluctantly, to welcome the priest as he came forward holding out his hands. The fine day blew across the forest and the bit of ground where three people had made their home, briefly enough in the fast flow of time. The little river, lacking rain, tinkled rather than gushed. On its banks the broom was in bright flower, particularly that fine bush from which Master Crespin had plucked a sprig to toss to Medley. Since he thrust it into the ground to keep green for a bit Medley had forgotten it. But now he saw, as he looked lingeringly over the place he must surely leave, that it had rooted and was growing. It showed green and vigorous. Next year it might flower.

8
Mallorys of Mantlemass

Medley slept in a small closet in the new wing of
Mantlemass that they had built after Dame Elizabeth
FitzEdmund died. The room was squeezed up in the
rafters. It was his own and therefore precious. Roger had
decided it should be Medley's place, that he shared with
no one, and there had been no dispute about it. There
was a small window and through it he looked out over
the farm buildings and the forest and beyond that to the
distant downs. It was an outlook utterly different from
the enclosed part of the forest he had known till now.
In the first months after his mother's death he had gone
back and back to Plashet's and wandered in and out of

the empty cottage, and found no comfort. But on All Souls day that year he had gone there for the last time. The cottage had been set on fire. The thatch and the rafters were burnt away, the chimney fallen, the four walls stood blackly against the misty winter weather. The little window that Dick Plashet had so cunningly made had shattered in the heat. Medley had scratched about in the ruins and the weeds to find something he might keep to remind him. He found the pane of glass with the top half of an unknown saint peering out. That was all that was left of his home.

His grandfather had made Medley a chest to fit under the window of his small room and hold his clothes. Sitting in his chair where his crippled state confined him, Tom Bostel had worked at a bench pulled across his knees. In the chest Medley kept two doublets handed down by Roger, three pairs of hose—one tidy, one so-so and one downright shabby—two pairs of shoes, three darned shirts that had belonged to one or other of the Mallorys, a pair of gloves made for him by Catherine's nurse Meg, and safe under all, his father's books. Hanging from one of the rafters, that their shape might be kept, were the riding boots Master Orlebar, Roger's godfather at Ghylls Hatch, had given Medley when he rode an unbroken colt for a bet and kept his seat. On the narrow sill under the window stood the piece of glass from Plashet's, a pot of ink, and a sheaf of quills stuck into a broken jar Medley had found up by the old road—it was certainly a Roman pot, Master Mallory said; old Sir James had told his pupils all about the Romans. Medley had never had so many possessions before and he still only half believed they were his. He had come to Mantlemass expecting to live with his grandfather and to work as one of fifty others about the farm all year long. He had faced the fact that this might mean the end of his friendship with Roger, for how could the master's son remain on familiar terms with one of his father's hinds— even if they had been schoolfellows? But when Lewis Mallory found the boy reading so fluently, and so proficient in Latin, he handed him over to Nicholas Forge, who had been secretary at Mantlemass since Dame Elizabeth's day, and was getting past the work. And he was glad enough to train up a pupil.

So Medley came to live in the big house, and wore a decent dark doublet and hose, and took pains to keep himself neat. He sat at table in the great hall with his immediate superior, with the steward and the bailiff, and opposite the older female servants, such as trusted Meg. The village priest, Sir Gregory, who was also chaplain to the manor, came most days for his dinner, sitting above Nicholas Forge, but below the younger Mallorys. This meant that Roger and he were side by side and talked together so much that Medley began to see Sir Gregory must indeed be wiser and more human than he had supposed before Anis's death. Indeed he had been almost as kind then as Sir James might have been, but Medley had resisted him for all that. He felt a little ashamed of his churlishness when he saw how eagerly the priest and Roger talked.

On occasion, Medley would be called from his place at table to wait upon Master Mallory—as he might be a page to some nobleman. In this way he learnt how to pour wine without clumsiness and attend to his master's wants, anticipating his wishes if possible, and all with quiet and courtesy. He was happy when he did this. He owed everything to this household, and so he made much of his service, growing more dexterous and neat each time, aware with pride that Catherine watched him. At

other times Roger was called upon to attend his father—
just as in London, in the household of Dame Cecily's
noble kinsman, Simon would have learnt the same service,
though in far grander surroundings.

Medley had been two years at Mantlemass when Simon
Mallory returned to his home. It was not only news of
his own fortunes that he brought, but news of the
King's death two days before, and of the accession of
his son.

'So now we have our eighth Henry,' Lewis Mallory
said. 'I pray God he be a good ruler to us.'

'He's a god!' cried Simon. 'A golden god!'

'An idol, then!' Dame Cecily cried, laughing.

'No, truly, madam—his hair is redly gold, his skin is
fair, his clothes are a splendour. He is learned and writes
poetry. He loves music. He sings and can play any
instrument you choose. He has even writ songs of his
own. He is pious and yet will dance the night through.
The ladies all love him for that, the men all love him
because he will hunt all day if need be. He is a paragon!'

'He'll never have time to govern the country,' Roger
said, 'with so much else to look after.'

'There speaks a yokel. You need to get yourself a little
worldly wisdom, brother, if you're to prosper.'

In the three years of his absence, Simon Mallory had
only been home once, and now it was hard to recognise
him. The boy had vanished, a man had taken his place.
He was tall, broad, grand in his manner. Medley, hovering
in the background of this conversation, waiting for his
master to sign some papers, and hoping he would not do
so too soon, wondered how Simon would ever settle down
to be lord of Mantlemass when it became his. This
exaggerated young gentleman seemed far from the lad
who had helped easily about the farm and made himself

8

the best thatcher of any. Now he seemed fitted to grace all the courts of Europe.

'Prosper where?' Roger was asking, quite gently. 'My plans are made and need no worldly wisdom to help me on.'

'Content to be an ignorant trader in excellent horses, are you?' mocked Simon.

'Like his father,' Lewis Mallory said quietly, glancing at his wife and grimacing slightly. 'I am sorry to know we all seem so rustic, Simon.' He turned to the hovering Medley and held out his hand. 'Are those for me?'

'Yes, sir. If you will sign, then Master Forge will set the seal.'

As he presented the papers, the pen and the ink pot, Medley knew that Simon was looking him up and down and he took care to avoid his gaze.

'There,' said Lewis Mallory, handing back the pen. 'See it gets on its way without too much delay or we shall lose a valuable sale. Does Master Orlebar know all the details set down here?'

'Yes, sir. I took a draft to Ghylls Hatch yesterday.'

'And you have made a very fair copy indeed. I wish I had your hand.' He smiled at Medley, handing back the paper. Medley knew he was dismissed and could hear no more of the talk. As he went to the door he heard Simon ask, 'Who's that?' And his father replied, 'In a few years from now I expect him to be my trusted secretary.'

'You've never forgotten Medley Plashet, brother?' Catherine cried.

'*Medley*! By'r Lady, I took him for some modest gentleman's son.'

Medley pulled the door hard behind him, but the thud that might have brought him a reprimand was prevented because Roger had risen from his place and followed, and he caught the door in time.

'When you've done with that letter,' he said easily, 'come outside and see what my brother has brought me from London. It is a fine hawk. A hobby, and well trained, he says.'

'A hobby for a young man,' said Medley. 'So what shall I have—a tercel for a poor man, or a kestrel for a servant?'

'Simon's grown spoilt and silly. He'll try to rule us all for a bit, but he'll soon tire.'

'If you say so,' said Medley. 'Sir.'

Roger cuffed him and pulled his hair over his eyes and went off laughing. If anyone knew how to preserve Medley's pride it was Roger, who seemed to need none of his own.

They flew the hobby next day, against Roger's inclination, for he knew he should give the bird time to know him. But Simon knew better—the bird was perfect because he said so and there could be no trouble. The others looked with awe at Simon's soft riding boots, his fringed gloves and the curled plume in his velvet cap. Even the dogs seemed impressed and kept their distance instead of bounding about boisterously, as Mantlemass dogs mostly did, eager, but willing to obey commands issued in the right voice—they cared most for Master Mallory.

Simon led out, with Roger behind, Catherine and Medley after that. Up on the highest ground, above the marsh where the old causeway ran that they were forbidden to ride, with heron fishing and kingfishers flashing through the reeds, they lost the hobby and argued hotly whose fault it had been, even Roger shouting in his fury and shaking his fist at Simon. Catherine was most disturbed for any harm that might come to the bird, flying off with jesses dangling, hampered in its flight and easily trapped by tangling branches. Her tenderness made Medley think of his mother, and how that very softness for dumb creatures had partly brought about her death. A great protective love for Catherine Mallory welled up in Medley, stronger because older than anything he had felt before. He rode home at her horse's flank, almost longing for some threat from which he might save her.

Catherine looked back over her shoulder. 'You ride like my squire, Medley.'

'So I am, lady,' he answered, 'and ever have been.'

'And surelye I were never better attended,' she said.

'Lord, lord,' groaned Simon. 'My sister's as rustic as a milkmaid. *Surelye I were!* You'll wed some farmer, Catherine, if you keep so far out of the decent world.'

'I'll wed when I choose—surelye,' said Catherine calmly. 'And it shall be who I choose and where I choose.'

'A maid shall go where her father and her brothers give her,' said Simon sharply. 'And that's all there is to say.'

Catherine curled her lip. 'Wait, then—and see if that is all there is to say.'

Later, when Medley was tidying away the day's work left lying by Nicholas Forge in the small chamber where they looked after the affairs of Mantlemass and Ghylls Hatch, Simon passed the open doorway, then returned to loll there watching and smiling his new, mocking smile.

'I see you have been fortunate since last we met,' he said.

'Have I so? I have lost both my father and my mother.'

'But you have found an easier way of life.'

'I have been helped in everything by my lord, your good father, and his lady wife. But I shall repay them.'

'Bravo! Fine words and finely spoken! You are certainly

learning,' said Simon. 'How shall you repay this debt you speak of?'

'With my life, if need be.'

'Oh, well done, indeed. They will like that better, I believe, than the sheep's eyes you cast after my sister.'

Medley did not answer, for he feared his own fury. To make an enemy of this changed Simon would be to sentence himself.

'You do not deny it, then?'

'I should scorn to,' said Medley, shrugging.

'Well, my little gentleman, I have warned you,' said Simon pleasantly. 'It might give me pleasure to thrash you—but pleasure or pain, I'll do it if I must . . . Now, a word in your ear. You are some years younger than I and have had no opportunity to learn the ways of the world. But I have learnt. I have learnt the dignity of blood and wealth. I pray you—remember that, and do not trespass on my father's generosity, or the generosity of any other Mallory.'

Medley was trembling with anger and humiliation. This was the first shadow cast on his time at Mantlemass. He hated Simon, and it was the first time he had hated. Why had he not stayed away for ever, or come back greater instead of mean and small? He had always been ready to chide and command the others, sometimes in a pompous manner, but most often in a quick-grinning, friendly way. If this was the way of life in the town and about the court, then Medley was content to stay in the country all the days of his life.

'I recall I have a message for you,' Simon said. 'I almost forgot. Seeing you here at Mantlemass quite sent it from my mind—I thought I should deliver it to a forest lad, not a household servant of my father's. A gentleman of sorts asked for you at my cousin's house.'

'For me?'

'He'd heard, he said, that there was one in the house who came from these parts. He asked if I knew of you.'

'You said—a gentleman of sorts . . . ?'

'A gentleman—but poor and even shabby. One Kit Crespin.'

'Master Crespin . . . He came once to Plashet's. He was my father's friend. It was a long time ago. Did he say so? Did he speak of my father?'

'Only of you. There is a look about him of evil times.'

'You have a message—that was what you said.'

'Call it a riddle. He told me to ask you if the sprig of broom has flowered.'

Medley was very still, his thoughts racing over this which seemed only one more riddle to add to all the rest.

'How am I to answer?'

'How indeed? You must wait till you make your next journey to London,' said Simon, laughing heartily at this idea. 'He's to be found, he said, at the Bear in Chepe, or at the old Tabard—which you are not likely to know is south of the river. So seek him there.'

'Perhaps I will—one day.'

'He's all of fifty years old. Best make haste, for I believe he is a gentleman not of fortune—but of misfortune . . . There, now. I have redeemed my pledge with much saving of time.' Simon still stayed where he was in the doorway, and by now he was looking at Medley in a narrow, speculative way. 'Has it?' he asked. 'The sprig of broom? Has it flowered?'

'It's not likely,' replied Medley, frowning. Was Master Crespin guessing, or did he somehow know that the broom had been planted and had taken root?

'The reply is as mysterious as the question. Both sound a little like passwords.'

Since Medley did not answer this, Simon shrugged and left him. Medley stayed where he was, shuffling through papers in a purposeless fashion. *A little like passwords* stayed in his mind, echoing as if it had been spoken in a lofty hall.

In June the new King was to be crowned, with his bride of two weeks, the Spanish princess Catherine. She had already come near the crown of England when she was married to the King's older brother Arthur, dead these several years. There was muttering about this first marriage, as to whether or not it was anything but a marriage in name, since the bride and groom had been so young; or whether indeed the new King was wedding his deceased brother's wife, which was against the laws of kinship and affinity laid down by the Church. When they talked of this at Mantlemass, Sir Gregory shook his head. Whether or not the Pope had given his blessing the situation could only be a dangerous one.

'They were children,' Dame Cecily said. 'Helpless victims of ambition. The tools of their parents . . .' She sounded very much moved, passionate indeed, as if the business were particularly near to her. And Medley recalled his grandfather telling him that the lady of Mantlemass had suffered greatly in childhood from her own father's ambitious scheming; she might have lost her happiness for ever, Tom Bostel had said, if she had not come to her aunt's house and found Lewis Mallory.

Whatever the rights and wrongs, the prognostications for happiness or disaster, the Mallorys would go to London to see the coronation. They would be guests of Lord Digby, that noble cousin of Dame Cecily's, from whose fine household Simon had just returned. From the moment that letters were exchanged, Mantlemass was turned upside down with the flurry of the arrangements.

'I call it a madhouse,' Medley told his grandfather. 'Dame Cecily pulls out gowns and veils and caps and petticoats, score upon score—and Master Lewis calls for order—and Catherine says they can never be in the fashion and must stay at home. Truly, grandfather, I doubt she wants much to go to London. She gets pretty miffed with the matter most days. Simon has clothes for a regiment, and Roger gets suited from his wardrobe. Simon tells his mother how this should be cut and that sewn, and Meg tries to do as he says and cockers it all up. Ask me, if they get to see the King it'll be the biggest miracle since any time.'

Now that Peg Bostel had left home and had her own household with Rufus Goodale, Tom Bostel had Meg's niece Judith to keep house for him. She was one of thirteen children, so homes had to be found for as many as possible. She was fifteen or so, very dark and quiet, and since she came Tom's cottage had shone and sparkled. He was growing fat, he grumbled, because she cooked so cunningly that a rabbit stew tasted like a dish of stuffed peacock. 'She'll make a fine wife for a good man,' Tom Bostel said—and repeated it every time Medley came viisting, and that was most days. Judith would stand rolling down her sleeves and looking at Medley till he smiled at her. Sometimes she smiled back and sometimes turned away as though she had not seen.

'She'd make a fine wife for *thee*,' Tom Bostel said at last, one day when she was out of the house. Then he looked keenly at his grandson and added, 'Unless thee's come too grand.'

Medley shook his head. Grandness had nothing to do with it. He liked Judith. If he were not allowed Catherine, then Judith would do—but only as well as the next girl.

'I don't aim to wed before twenty at least,' he muttered. 'Come old Nick goes I'll be secretary, and that's a fine thing. He's promised it.'

In the third week of June, Medley stood to watch the Mallorys come out of the house to their waiting horses, two pack mules and six servants. It was a small enough train, but all he could or would afford, so Master Mallory had said. Until the very last moment Medley had hoped a miracle might happen and there would be a place for him. Perhaps more than anything he longed to seek out Master Crespin 'at the Bear in Chepe, or at the old Tabard, south of the river', for he might be able to tell something of his father. As Roger was on the point of leaving, Medley told him about Master Crespin, so that if opportunity should arise he might look for him.

Now the whole train was mounted and farewells were cried. Medley ran out on to the forest track to get a last glimpse of them. Catherine had seemed to avoid looking at him, but he knew she never liked to say goodbye. Now suddenly she turned in her saddle and waved.

He stood a long time listening as the sound of the horses died away, then ran round to the other side of the house and watched the cavalcade pass through a gap between the trees, just where the track turned and made for the London road. He waved vigorously, almost desperately, but this time no one waved back. An immense silence settled then over all his world. There was a mist over the sun that day and the forest hardly breathed. The trees seemed as if painted on the sky, then smudged by a careless hand. Birds were silent. No shouting man, no barking dog, not even the rustle of a passing deer or rabbit or even mouse touched or disturbed the utter stillness.

'Come you along in, now, Medley Plashet!' Meg called

from the doorway. 'I dunnamany days we'll wait to see 'em back. But time goes, willy nilly.'

Medley heard himself give a sort of groan. Meg laughed, but kindly, and he turned red. He passed her as he went into the house, and she touched his arm gently, almost consolingly. She knew too much, he thought, and wondered uneasily if he had not been taken in attendance because already they had decided to keep Catherine and him apart.

Down in the village there was dancing on the green to honour the coronation of King Henry VIII, with a maypole slightly out of season, and morris men with jingling bells and coloured ribbons. Tom Bostel told Medley he should take Judith to see the fun, but Medley felt mopey and found other things to do. Then, when the rest had gone off chattering together across the forest, he felt very melancholy and ill-tempered indeed. He stood in the June dusk, sick with his own frustrations, and saw the distant downs sharp with points of light where loyal countrymen set great beacons flaming for the King. All that was unhappy in Medley's life—his position in law, the loss of his father, his mother's death, and now the distance set between him and Catherine Mallory, moved him almost to despair. For it was most bitterly true that the better his own immediate situation, the more he saw with the eyes and accepted opinions of those he lived among. He was not nearer to Catherine for being better fed and clothed, his work acceptable and his future promised. Instead, increasingly he was aware of a trust that he should not betray, and saw himself more and more as her parents must see him, even if she seemed not to see him thus herself. By consorting with them he began to understand their attitudes and interpretations, which instead of bringing him closer could only set him

farther apart. That 'dignity of blood and wealth' of which
Simon had boasted, seemed likely to choke and stifle
Medley, putting an end to all his dearest hopes.

Two weeks passed and there was no news of the family
save a letter sent from Master Lewis to Nicholas Forge.
This concerned only plans for the harvest, a query about
the hay crop, just then in the cutting, and an order to
send three heifers to market. Medley made excuses to
ride to Ghylls Hatch, for old Roger Orlebar would always
talk about the Mallorys. Lewis Mallory had been his
ward, so perhaps he knew him better than any other
living man. Master Orlebar would tell tales of Dame
Elizabeth FitzEdmund, who had made Mantlemass a
great and respected manor. Particularly he loved to speak
of Roger, his godson, of his ease with horses that was as
fine as his father's. Orlebars had been at Ghylls Hatch
for many years now, but when he found his first vigour
going Roger Orlebar had given the place to Lewis
as a trust for Roger.

'A man may die easy, knowing who shall inherit,' said
Master Orlebar. 'I have often thought shame to have no
son of my own—but these two are my children.'

As if Medley was the next best thing to Roger, being
always so close to him, Master Orlebar let him ride the
grandest horses that he owned, and complimented him
on his skill in handling them.

'It was not for nothing I gave you those boots,' he
said. 'When Roger comes to Ghylls Hatch in due time,
it seems to me you should be his right-hand man.'

Because of his loneliness at this time, Medley also
talked more than before to the priest, and every day
respected him more. Sir Gregory had the outward appearance of a sturdy, dark-browed peasant, his blood almost
alien in this part of the country, but his mind had a

quality and a depth that made his devotion to his calling almost poetic.

However much he fretted at the Mallorys' absence, this time was not wasted for Medley.

Then one cool pink evening, as Medley rode home to Mantlemass by way of the high road above the village, a horseman overtook him—and there was Roger.

Medley was so glad to see him that for a second or two he could not speak, but stared at him and grinned like a fool, his mouth so stretched with pleasure he felt he might never be able to close it again.

'You look like a Hallowe'en turnip,' Roger said.

'Lord, I've missed the sight of you!' Medley managed. 'How was it? Did you see the King?'

'We were at court, friend—so I could not miss him. Simon was right to call him golden—the golden Harry, you hear men say . . . There was a great banquet, and afterwards His Grace led out my mother in a galliard. Well, I think it were a galliard.'

Medley smiled again. 'You've not changed. Simon changed.'

'Save us all, I was only there some weeks! For all that,' said Roger, 'you know I do not change. Come on— lead me home. I'm sore sick of being away.'

It was only as they moved off side by side that Medley quite realised no others of the party had come up with them.

'Has no one else come home to Mantlemass?'

'Tomorrow. I came ahead for my own good reasons . . . Medley, you must get that look out of your eyes—it may lead to trouble.'

'What look—?'

'I have three things to tell you. You'd better know first that my sister stays on in London for a time.' He

looked at Medley and muttered, 'I might as well have
told you she is dead, the way you look.'

'How long a time?' Medley asked.

'A month, perhaps. Well—she's young, Melly. She
needs to see how the world goes. There's much gaiety to
be seen in London.'

'Do you mean, Roger, that they are finding her a
husband?'

'She will be courted—that's for sure. But nothing shall
be against her will. You know my mother is strong about
that—she suffered too much herself ever to forget it.
Nothing against her own good wishes, Melly.'

Did that make it all seem much better or much worse?
Medley was uncertain.

'What else? You said three things.'

'I have come to a decision I've delayed too long. I once
said I might not be either lord or lackey. Do you recall
that?'

'Something—'

'I have decided to enter the Church.'

This time Medley was completely stunned. Certainly
Roger had had his moments of withdrawn seriousness—
but they had never lasted long. He had appeared no
holier than the next of them when it came to prayers and
church services. Medley checked himself there, for he
recalled how latterly when Sir Gregory came to say Mass
at the manor chapel, and the boys were to take it in turns
to act as server, Roger had relieved Medley time and
again and left him to sleep. In such moments, then, he
must have come to his immense decision.

'Well—do you wish me a good life?' Roger asked.

'I shall do—indeed I shall do. Only now I can only
see I've lost my friend.'

'No, no,' said Roger lightly, 'you've won an advocate

with heaven! Think how I'll pray for you and see your soul safe hereafter!'

It seemed strange to hear him mock so vast a matter.

'Cheer up, Melley Plashet. Wait long enough and I'll be ordained priest and marry you to your lady.'

'That's years ahead.'

'Be patient, then.'

'Where will you go?'

'If I am accepted—to the Benedictines at St Pancras Priory.'

'When?'

'When I have courage to tell my news at home. Except Sir Gregory, you're the first I've told.'

'Master Orlebar's going to take it hard.'

'I'll take it hard there, too, Medley. I did yearn after Ghylls Hatch.'

'Must you, Roger? Are you sure of it?'

'Certain sure . . . Come on—stop maundering there and let's get home. I'll beat you to it.'

He rode off fast, but Medley had not the spirit to follow. His whole future seemed changed by a few words given in confidence. His horse fretted, seeing the other ahead, and at last he let it go. Roger was waiting for him at the next crossing.

'I didn't tell you the third thing. I sought out your Master Crespin, as you ordered.'

Medley brisked up a bit. 'Yes? Well? Did you find him?'

'News of him.'

'Go *on!*'

'He'd been lodged at the Tabard some months, they told me there.'

'Had been?'

'It seems he's now lodged somewhere very different.'

Roger frowned and looked at Medley in a puzzled way. 'What do you know of him?'

'Nothing but his face, and his fine horse and clothes. And his friendship with my father. It seemed they'd known one another many years . . . But Simon spoke as if he'd fallen on evil times.'

'Indeed they are evil,' Roger said. 'Three weeks ago he was arrested and taken to the Tower.'

9
Kit Crespin

Of the news that Roger brought home from London, that concerning Master Crespin was the most confusing. Not to see Catherine in her place at Mantlemass was grievous and full of implied danger; to lose Roger seemed like the threat of losing a right hand; but that Master Kit Crespin, so little known, so clearly recollected, should be held in the Tower of London took Medley's breath away. How important a man, then, was his father's old friend? He had seemed unattached, without family, a man to be enquired for at inns—and Simon had described him as a 'gentleman of misfortune'. Simon had assuredly been right. Yet he could be no common criminal, no debtor, murderer or swindler, or he would have been put away elsewhere. The Tower stood for treason, above all else. What treason had Kit Crespin committed, and what might happen to him? What might be happening to him now? Medley thought of him constantly.

After six weeks there was no word of Catherine, and Dame Cecily began to fret.

'My cousin Digby faithfully promised to send word often.'

'You cannot expect a messenger every week,' her husband said.

'Then the messenger must be ours. It is time she came home. I need her here.'

He laughed a little. 'She is not a baby.'

'You have forgotten!' Dame Cecily said, quite sharply. 'You know I shall never see my daughter treated by her parents as I was treated—I will not abandon her among strangers.'

They were at table with all the rest, but he laughed as gently and fondly as if they had been alone in their own chamber. 'Ah, but remember what the strangers brought you,' he said. 'Your husband and your household!'

'Let no stranger present my daughter with a husband and a household! Not unless it be with her wish and consent.'

'Keep that from your fine cousin,' he advised. 'They will surely think you a madwoman. A wench is no more than a wench, they'll say. As your father did. What has changed? In that world—nothing.'

'But for my Catherine—everything!' she said fiercely, and beat with the flat of her hand upon the table. Medley was pouring the wine that day, and he was standing just then at Dame Cecily's shoulder. He saw how tautly she held herself, and her hands were shaking as she took

9

up her wine. 'We'll send tomorrow,' she said; and looked at her husband with a challenging expression that made her eyes flash finely.

Simon was watching his mother, half in disapproval and half in amusement at her rage.

'I'll ride to London, madam.'

'No, indeed, you shall not! We know your way of thinking, sir. You'd sell your sister to the highest bidder.'

'I cannot spare a man until we've seen the harvest home,' Lewis Mallory said. 'Your cousin will surely send very shortly. A man who keeps his London house has no call to be bothered with the harvest.'

'Codlins and pippins and a few small herbs,' Dame Cecily said dismissively. 'That's the London harvest— the rest must be marketed. It's a false way of living.'

At this Master Mallory guffawed into his beard and took her hand and kissed it. 'God bless you, wife,' he said, 'you are a true countrywoman. I honour you for it. But as a countrywoman you must respect the harvest here. If there's no word from your cousins once the corn's cut and carried—then I promise I'll spare a messenger.'

That year more land had been cleared. All of it had been sown and must now be cropped, though next year two-thirds would lie fallow in preparation for the following season. Over the whole manor the crop was a heavy one—wheat and barley and oats, all to be safely garnered, according to long custom, by the feast of the Assumption of Our Lady. Everyone was needed that year to bring the harvest home, and Simon put off his fine clothes, and his finer manner, and sweated with the rest. Medley thought he seemed glad to do so. He, too, was glad to leave his work with Nicholas Forge and labour all day in the sun and wind. He carried his grandfather out of

doors, too, for Tom Bostel could not stomach his own
idleness at such a time, and set him on a bench where
he could watch the cutting on the far bank. The neighbouring stretch had been cut and set up in sheaves
already, and now the oxen came and went, dragging the
loads to the barnyard for threshing. Peg came to Mantlemass, along with her old husband, and all those tenants
from the forest and the village who owed service to the
manor. The weather was fine, the work seemed endless.
Roger said he must wait till harvest home to tell his
father of his decision.

'Wait till Michaelmas, wait till the fruit's in,' Medley
urged.

'And then wait till Martinmas for the last root and
berry, I suppose!'

'I shall be alone when you go.'

'You'll never be alone at Mantlemass,' said Roger,
'and you know it. I'll not stoop to pity you!' They were
resting briefly on a great pile of last year's straw, raked
out of the barn to make way for fresh. 'Come on, you
gurt grummut,' growled Roger, in the voice he had not
used a long while now. 'Give over grizzling, do, and get
thee armed-up. There's naun won wi'out a battle.'

The hot sun stayed to help on the heavy days. Towards
the end they were already looking with satisfaction and
pleasure at the results of their labour. Barns and granaries
would be generously stocked this winter, and the fruit
promised as well as the grain. When the last sheaf was
carried they wiped their brows, washed their hands and
gave thanks. That was in the evening, and next morning,
as if he had been waiting out of sight, Lord Digby's
messenger rode in to Mantlemass.

There were two letters. The first from his lordship
told of the good health of his young cousin, who 'is

become a goodly part of our household by this'. The second was crumpled and dirty, and the messenger brought it out stealthily and handed it over with a great air of guilt. He had promised to deliver it, he said, but without the knowledge of his master. It was for Dame Cecily.

'Madam,' ran the scrawl, 'save me I hat my cozins and have bin beat. I must die I com not hom to ye.'

'*Now* will you send?' Dame Cecily cried.

'Roger shall go,' said Master Lewis. He looked both distressed and angry. 'But see you enquire discreetly, Roger. Your sister is still a child and has a child's impatience. I am very loath to offend his lordship.'

'I am very ready to offend his lordship's lady!' retorted his wife. 'If I learn she has truly beaten my Kitten I'll have the hair from her scalp!' Then she wept and clasped Roger round the neck and implored him to go and fetch his sister home, without ado or delay.

'Trust me, mother,' Roger said, kissing her cheek. 'I'll ride at once after dinner. Who shall you spare to go with me, sir? Let it be Medley Plashet.'

His father said without hesitation that it should be so. 'He must needs learn the road to London. Nicholas Forge will soon be past the ride. It will be for you to act for me then, Medley, in the affairs of the manor. Keep your wits about you as you go. Look around and see what you can learn . . . Well, what do you say to all this?' he demanded. Stunned both by hearing what Catherine had written and by the prospect of going at last to London, Medley stared at him helplessly.

He and Roger rode out shortly after noon. The day was overcast with a hint of thunder. They went by Ghylls Hatch, where Roger begged his godfather for a better mount for Medley.

'Take Cynthus,' the old man said. 'He's steady and a sweet ride. Cherish him. If you do other I'll surely punish you when you get back.'

'I am wearing my boots that you gave me,' Medley pointed out. 'You know why you gave 'em, sir. Not for riding ill!'

It was good to set out on a journey with Roger, a longer one than they had ever made. Time to talk and the energy to ride hard, and an air of expectancy and drama and anxiety over all to spur them to London. They rode high on the forest ridge, descended into flat country for some miles, then began again to approach hilly country. Medley had never seen so much of the world before. Everywhere the harvest was just ending; men, women and children were labouring. The children gleaned over the stubble fields, their faces reddened by the sun. On every hill, or so it seemed, a windmill stood, already working on the winter's store. Along the road the villages came one by one, sturdy dwellings, solid churches, farms and manors that all seemed to Medley most wonderful. Yet it seemed strange to him that people lived thus so openly, so far from the shelter of the forest, their houses exposed to all the traffic on the road, to the dust kicked up by passing horses, by trundling carts and the shuffle of oxen.

'Where shall we lie tonight?' asked Medley. 'Shall it be at an inn?'

'It shall. And leave gawping like a bumpkin,' said Roger, mocking. 'Take things as they come and time shall make you a gentleman, will you, nil you.'

'I pray so,' said Medley, grinning in his turn. 'What inn shall it be?' He only knew the two that Master Crespin had named to Simon, the Bear and the Tabard.

'I'd say the Tabard,' Roger said. 'Two birds and one

stone. They'll tell you anything they know of your father's friend.'

Again the day seemed to intensify. The clouds came lower, lightning showed the horizon, a promise of the storm that might break later and cleanse the air.

As they came nearer London the traffic increased, and there was some waiting and some jostling at narrow bridges and at fords. Roger grew impatient, but Medley was too amazed to bother. He had never seen so many riding at one time, nor so many waggons drawn by great-shouldered horses. There was a hurry over them all, too, that was quite unfamiliar to him. All seemed bent upon business that could not wait. It might have been the salvation of their immortal souls that concerned them so deeply—but Roger said it was more surely some affair of trade and commerce; nothing counted in London, he said, but trade and wealth and rank, to which all else must be subservient.

When they came to the inn at last it was after dark. The yard was jostling with people, bright with torches flaring in their iron sconces against the walls. Servants ran hither and yon, shouted at and shouting. Everyone spoke so strangely that Medley was utterly confused. Roger's ear seemed better tuned, and he began shouting in his turn, bellowing for an ostler. A lad appeared at last and led the way to the stables. He would have taken the horses himself, but Roger did not trust him. He and Medley watched that the horses were fed and watered, then Roger slipped the ostler a coin.

'See them kept fast or I'll put the watch on you,' he threatened. 'I know how easily a good horse may be lost . . . Inn stables are notorious, Medley. Leave a fine beast at midnight and find a nag at noon.'

'The Tabard's got a good name, sir,' said the ostler,

'these hundred year and more. Trust me, sir. Just ask for Ned. Where do you aim to sleep, gentlemen?'

'In the loft,' said Roger firmly. 'See there's enough straw for good bedding, Ned. Now—supper.'

He strode off as confidently as if he had been travelling the world for years on end. Medley followed, speechless from shyness, confusion at the bustle—and sheer admiration of Roger's bold manner.

'Have you slept often at an inn?' he asked, and he sounded so respectful that Roger gave a snort of laughter.

'Once. Now look about you, Medley. You will come this way yourself often enough in the future.'

While they were at supper the landlord was going the rounds of that night's guests. Many of them he greeted as old friends, matching his manner to their status, made obvious by the quality of their dress. The noise under the low-raftered ceiling was almost overwhelming, and it was not helped by the thick smoky atmosphere. Each newcomer must shout to make himself heard, and the din in the yard seemed to suggest that horses, men and dogs were engaged in endless battle.

'A full house, landlord,' Roger said.

'It's the King's crowning, and all the people in London for it. There's still coming and going all the time. Do you cross the river come morning?' He looked more closely at Roger. 'I think you come here afore, young sir.'

'Can you be certain?'

'A trick o' the trade, remembering faces, sir. You asked for Master Kit Crespin.'

'I did. On behalf of my friend here. Tell him what you told me.'

The landlord gave his attention to Medley for the first time. He said in an astonished voice, 'He never did tell he had a son.'

'I'm not his son,' said Medley, startled.

'You have a good look of him, whether or not you say so.' And he winked first at Roger, then at Medley.

'We are no kin,' Medley insisted. As he spoke he remembered what he had utterly forgotten—that his father and Master Crespin had themselves seemed not unlike.

'As well for you, I daresay,' the landlord said. 'Master Crespin has come on evil times.' He moved closer and spoke behind his hand. 'I told you, sir,' he said to Roger, 'that they hauled him off to the Tower. Now I say worse. He's mortal sick and bound to die there.'

'How do you know this?'

'I'm his supplier. He'd starve fast enough without I took him rations. I or one of my sons goes three times a week before noon. As many another poor prisoner's friend does, too. But it's my sorry guess we'll be quit of our trouble soon enough.' He looked again at Medley. 'Do you wish to see the gentleman?'

Medley clenched his hands to stop them shaking. 'How?'

'Like any other. Open your purse.' The landlord gave a kind of laugh. 'There's prisoners and prisoners. You'll not find him in a dungeon shackled by the leg.'

'When do you go next?'

'Tomorrow,' the landlord said.

They crossed the river in good time. Peter, the landlord's second son, went with them. Roger would go to his cousin's house, taking the horses with him, and Medley would follow him later. There was a mist over the river, but the sun glittered through it and, as they crossed, the Tower swam up ahead of them like a great ship at anchor. Then as the mist peeled away from the walls the illusion faded. Harsh stone on stone, the palace, fortress, prison displayed without compromise its crushing strength.

Once parted from Roger, Medley seemed to move into a world of nightmare. About the steps by the outer wall, where barges tied up, were many people coming and going, and others loitering, purposeful yet idle, both men and women, and sometimes women with children by them.

'They may get to see their men,' said Peter. 'Or not. As the warders fancy.'

'Will it be so for us?'

'No. For a warder here is my uncle,' the landlord's son replied. 'This helps our trade.' He looked impatient as Medley stared. 'We're suppliers to more than Master Crespin. You might say we have a licence. Well—there's many after it, and they all pay up,' he said crossly. 'It's profit, see? Lord, what a yokel! What a bumpkin you are, young sir. Did you think it was all for love of Master Crespin?'

Medley did not answer. Peter was fat, his eyes and his mouth were small and greedy. Medley followed him and did as he was told, sitting in a boat that swam in by dark dripping walls to slippery steps, and moving off along passages that echoed. He was afraid of what he might see. Yet curiously, as they were led deeper into the great building, there came to seem a kind of grisly sociability about the place in this quarter. Gaolers and callers seemed on the best of terms and sometimes coin chinked on coin. Was it known, Medley wondered, that this traffic took place, or would it one day cease abruptly, with all that must mean for those awaiting help?

That day it was not Peter's uncle who unlocked the door for them, and so the tale had to be told of the rest of the family being sick and the stranger kindly helping out.

'Show me the basket, then,' said the turnkey. 'No knives, I trust, or weapons? No phials of poison or drugs or magic charms? No disguises?'

'None, sir,' said Peter sniggering.

'I'll take the pie for myself,' the man said.

After this they passed through a number of doors that must be unlocked then locked again. Then they came to a narrow curving corridor, where the walls were drier. Here were many locked doors with grilles set into them, from which a face at times looked out.

'One, today,' the gaoler said, pausing at last and swinging his keys.

Peter thrust his own basket on Medley's free arm. 'I'll be here when you come out.'

Within was less a prison cell, as imagination had shown it, than a small cramped room lit by a narrow barred window, and with some pretence at furnishing. There was a table, a chair, a small closet. The bed had curtains, though they were dirty and tattered. The room was both cold and airless. It smelt, Medley knew at once, of death, but whether past or to come he would not have been able to say.

Kit Crespin was lying on the bed in his shirt and hose. His beard had grown and it jutted upward because his head was thrown far back. He had been sleeping, perhaps. He did not move at the sound of the door unlocked then locked again, but merely opened his eyes.

'Tom or Peter?' he asked, in a stronger voice than Medley had expected from the looks of him.

'Neither, sir,' said Medley.

'Who?' He pulled himself up on his elbow. 'Who, then?'

Medley moved nearer, not knowing what to say, frightened and shocked and angered all at once. The change in the man was so great. He looked old, so old, his skin drained and colourless, his eyes enormous. They stared at one another, and Medley tried again. 'Medley Plashet, Master Crespin,' he said.

There was a long, long pause. Crespin looked Medley in the eyes, and then his gaze travelled over his face, then covered him from top to toe.

'Great God Almighty,' he said very softly. 'The sprig of broom . . .'

Medley could no longer contain the depth of his feeling for one so nearly a stranger, so entirely a friend. He knelt down by the bed and took Master Crespin's hand. 'Why are you so sick? Why are you here?'

'I am sick because I am here. I am here for safety's sake—but not my own.'

'What will happen?'

'They'll not harm me, if that is what you mean. Gallows and scaffolds take time and money. I'm not worth it. They'll let me die. That's easy.'

'If I might understand, sir—'

'Nothing I can tell you, boy. I swore that to your father long ago . . . You had better not have come. There's still one to watch. He was here—was it yesterday? See no one follows when you leave . . .'

He must be rambling, Medley thought, so he frowned but did not answer.

'Have you spoken to your father, Medley Plashet?'

'He went away. It was a long time ago. My mother died. I live at Mantlemass.'

'Richard went into Kent . . . Your father went into Kent. He works as a mason. He has yet another name . . .

There was a lad from Mantlemass I asked for news of you—when was that?'

'It was when the King was crowned.'

'I asked if the sprig of broom had flowered.'

At this moment Peter hissed outside the grille and said, 'You must hurry, if there's much more you want to say.'

'Next year, perhaps, Master Crespin. I did plant it, and it grows very stoutly. I had your message.'

'Tell your father—there is only one left. Tell him from me. Remember that.'

Peter now beat with his palm on the door. 'Hurry!' Far away down the long passage there was some sound.

'*There is only one left*,' Medley repeated, more to humour the sick man than for any other reason that he could see. Then something leapt clear into his mind. 'Only one of the three strangers,' he stated. 'They came a second time, and then my father went away.'

'Proudless is the name,' murmured Crespin, tiring now, lying back with his eyes shut and breathing very noisily. 'Safe soon,' he said. 'All of us.'

Did he mean safe in death? And *All of us*? How many, and who?

'Sir—Master Crespin—can you not see a physician?'

'Too late.' Then he opened his eyes and took Medley by the arm and said strongly, 'I shall tell you one thing— find him to know the rest. We shared a father, he and I. Half-brothers—though our mothers would never have met in this life, that's sure.'

'I look like you,' Medley managed to reply, amazed enough, yet seeing a thing or two more clearly. 'The landlord at the Tabard thought I was your son.'

'Well, I like the idea,' said Crespin, raising up from somewhere that quick, quirky smile that Medley had never forgotten. 'But I have been wiser than your father. I have never acknowledged any son of mine.'

Now Medley could hear doors opened and shut, and voices. Again Peter thumped and called to him.

'I have to say farewell, sir.'

'Farewell, nephew,' said Kit Crespin so quietly that only Medley close beside him could have heard. 'Greet my brother from me.' He turned his face away and closed his eyes. 'Proudless,' he said.

Then the key slotted into the lock and the door was flung open. With terrible reluctance Medley turned away and dragged himself through the door. His thoughts and his affections seemed to be torn out of him as he turned his back on Kit Crespin, knowing he would never see him again.

Outside, the mist had cleared and the sun shone over the huge, fine building, setting a gloss upon its burden of cruel secrets. The river sparkled, gay and crowded with barges, for the air of holiday induced by the excitements of the coronation still hung over London. There was still about the outer walls of the tower keep, too, that shifting, aimless crowd whose business could only be conjectured. A man there moved out of the press and called to Peter. 'You, there! Peter! Is he still alive?'

Medley swung on his heel at the sound. The voice struck some faint far echo in his mind and he peered against the sun to see the man who had shouted. Peter pulled him on.

'A Tower raven,' he said. 'Relations wait for the pickings when their prisoners die.'

'Who's he, though—that knows Master Crespin?'

'I never put a name on him.' Peter looked at Medley and pulled a face. 'Is all well with you? You're the colour of green cheese. The Tower can make a man puke that

never went inside before . . . Can you find your way
now?'

'Which way for Blackfriars?'

'Upstream a little.'

'Thanks for your help. When you see him next—'

'Be dead b'nightfall. The Tower squeezes men to
death. Master Crespin lived hard and he'll die easy.'

'Easy—?'

'Easier than many.' Peter still lingered, walking along
beside Medley, waiting for something. At last Medley
pulled out the only money he had, which was a noble, and
Peter snatched it and was gone.

Medley moved away slowly down the hill. Then he
paused and looked back, puzzled by the man who had
called out, by that hint of familiarity that he could not
chase through his memory. Through the coming and
the going on the hill he thought he saw the man moving
leisurely. He saw his face quite clearly, and again was
puzzled out of his wits by some likeness. The wildest
conjecture suddenly turned him cold—that this was the
only one left, and that he recalled the voice because he
had indeed heard it before, though so long ago. He
remembered Kit Crespin telling him to be sure he was
not followed. He quickened his step almost to a run.
Then the sunlight and the ordinary, cheerful men and
women among whom he moved, made his imaginings
seem absurd. He looked back once more, and saw no
sign of pursuit. He straightened his shoulders, then, and
steadied his step.

Presently the fine houses began, with gardens running
green and flowery to the water's edge. Though he was
lost as soon as found, Master Crespin was the only
kin beside his parents that Medley had ever known, and
strangely this fact seemed to add to his stature. He lifted

his head and walked more firmly, and when he enquired of a passer-by for Lord Digby's house, his voice was strong and unexpectedly commanding. Not that that did him much good, for he had to speak a second and a third time, and very slowly, to make himself understood—and then had some difficulty himself with the reply.

He found the place at last. This was the house, Roger had told him, where Sir Thomas Jolland, Dame Cecily's father, had kept her close in girlhood. After his death she had not cared to own it, but had made a sale of it to her Digby cousins. The high studded gates were open into the wide courtyard. Medley found himself annoyed that he came on foot like anybody's hired messenger. He was glad to see the horses tethered in the yard, at the foot of the stairs leading up to a little gatehouse. A porter came out and challenged Medley. As he replied that he sought Master Roger Mallory, the horses pricked their ears at the sound of his familiar voice, and Cynthus turned his head and snorted grandly. The porter seemed to bow a little.

At this moment, the great door of the house opened, and a whole knot of people streamed through and spread over the steps. There were loud voices and protests. Six or seven servants flurried uncertainly about an angry man, who must be their master, while two young girls wept and one fine lady scolded furiously. In the midst walked Roger holding Catherine by the hand.

Medley froze at the sight of her—pale and thin, her face blotched as though she had wept for days. Unable to check himself, he ran forward.

'Get the horses, Medley,' Roger called. 'Take my sister with you on Cynthus. I'll say good-day to you, cousins. Good-day, my lord.'

A great babble of fury and protest broke out again.
Medley heard little of it, for Catherine gave the final
touch to the general scandal by breaking away from her
brother and running to Medley with both her arms
stretched out to him in welcome.

10

Catherine

They hired a third horse at the Tabard and rode home
slowly, staying overnight at a convent guesthouse fifteen
miles out of London. All that time Catherine barely spoke
save *Yes* and *No*. In the morning she had recovered her
spirits. For the rest of the way she gabbled excitedly
about the vagaries and cruelties and stupidities of her
Digby cousins, and how she would never again in all her
life go to London or to any town or city, but would
live peaceably in the countryside and speak how she
chose—saying *miffed* and *maundering, stoachy* and *spilt*
and *dunnamany* as much and as often as ever she thought
she would.

'They never even heard half the words I know,' she said with contempt. 'There was my cousin Jane was doing her tapestry, and there was a line should go skitter-waisen, and so I said it should go. And how she did laugh! A high, silly laugh Jane has, too. "Oh, come quick, sister," she cry out to my cousin Kate. "Listen how this girl speaks so outlandish—like a savage out of the forest." And Cousin Kate said, "So she is." And so,' said Catherine, 'like a savage out of the forest I was bound to behave.'

'Sister Puss Mallory,' said Roger very soberly, 'I came to London to save you and brought you away in great anger because of your pale face and tearful eyes. But have you after all been simply wicked and earned your just reward?'

'I'll tell all another time,' muttered Catherine. She glanced at Medley. She was still very pale, her eyes glittering but deeply shadowed. '*He* believes me,' she said. '*He* trusts what I say.' Her eyes suddenly filled with tears again, and she turned away her head. 'What shall my father say to me?' she cried in a voice of misery.

They rode up to Mantlemass in the late afternoon. Roger lifted Catherine from the saddle, and with his arm firmly about her led her towards the house. Then Meg came rushing out and the tears were all to do again.

Medley watched them through the door and heard Dame Cecily's voice, and then Master Lewis himself rode in from the forest.

'Well?' he asked, as he dismounted.

'Her brother's brought her home, sir.'

'Take Diana, Medley,' Master Lewis said, and went quickly indoors.

Medley was left with all four horses and shouted for help and a boy ran out of the stables and led the animals

away. Medley did not know what to do next. With the
business of Catherine coming on top of his encounter
with Kit Crespin in the Tower, he was in turmoil twice
over. He was convinced, now, that he must somehow
find his father, that the time had come when he must
demand to know more than he had been allowed to know.
To do this he must have permission to leave Mantlemass
for an unspecified time—a day or two, a year, he could
not tell how long. If that permission were refused, and
why indeed should it be granted, then he must choose
between seeking out his father and remaining at least
within the orbit of those he loved . . . Meanwhile his
immediate problem was how to learn what Catherine was
telling of her time in London, how her parents were
receiving her. He had no place in the family councils and
could not burst into the winter parlour, or wherever they
were talking together, to listen and to comment. He must
wait until Roger told him what had taken place—and
Roger would tell him, for he understood everything
Medley thought and felt.

As he stood hesitating, wondering if he should go to
his grandfather's cottage to tell of his safe return, Meg
called to him from the doorway.

'Come you in, boy. Master Lewis needs you.'

Medley ran indoors, so abruptly that Meg had to call
after him, 'In the parlour! Take ink and paper, he say.'

When Medley got to the parlour, and he was there
within seconds, Master Lewis was standing by the window; Catherine sat beside her mother on the settle, and
Roger had perched himself on the table corner. Simon
was not present, he was away on manor business; however
much Simon had improved lately, Medley was greatly
relieved that he was elsewhere. The atmosphere, which he
had feared to find angry, seemed more distressed than

anything. Lewis Mallory turned from the window as Medley came in. His face was stern but there was certainly no true anger there.

'Sit at the table, Medley,' he said, 'and write a letter as I shall tell you. It goes to my Lord Digby. It shall be brief, I promise. Write it as you please, then make me a fair copy to sign. And my daughter shall sign it, too.'

'I will not,' said Catherine.

'You shall say you are sorry for your discourtesy: no more, no less.'

'I am not sorry.'

'Now, Catherine,' said her mother. 'By your own account you have deserved something of the treatment you received. But only something,' she added, firm and sharp, so that the likeness between mother and daughter suddenly intensified. 'My cousin's wife may not indeed have beaten you—as you naughtily claimed—'

'She skreeled at me and boxed my ears!'

'I think she was provoked.'

'Are you ready, Medley?' Master Lewis asked.

'Indeed, sir.' Medley glanced quickly at Roger, and Roger shrugged and pulled a face. Perhaps he had been blamed for bringing his sister away from London with so little ceremony.

'She made me eat bread and water,' Catherine cried.

'Childish behaviour merits childish punishment.'

'And she had chosen me a husband!'

At this the atmosphere noticeably quickened.

'What husband, pray?' her mother asked.

'Whose daughter are you—his or mine? Your cousin does presume, I think, madam,' Master Lewis said to Dame Cecily.

'It's his wife at the bottom of all,' she answered, her voice cold with dislike.

'Who were you to marry, Puss?' Roger asked.

'Why, Lady Susannah's own brother. And he's an old man of thirty and has one wife dead already and seven children from her. But they said she had been a person of little importance and the children should be sent away. And the eldest,' Catherine rushed on, 'is a girl one year older than me, and is to be married. But only to the steward's son. Which is shocking, my cousins said. "Oh— why so?" said I. "Why does she marry him, then?" And my cousin Jane laughed cruelly and said, "She say— says—she loves him. And that's an indecent thing any- way," my cousin say—says.'

'Oh, Catherine, how you do gabble and gossip,' her mother said. 'What are we to believe?'

'You are to believe me, madam,' Catherine said. She sat up straight and stiff at her mother's side, and gripped her two hands tightly together on her knee. She looked straight ahead of her with those feverish eyes and said quite slowly, and so clearly that every word rang in the pleasant room, 'I wished her joy, that girl. *I* was not shocked. For why must she marry any but the one she love? One day she must've spoke out loud and said *I love him and I'll be his wife, gentleman or no gentleman.* And that,' said Catherine, her breath almost going on the last words, 'is what I'll do. And say right out—I hated them because I feared they could make me wed without you knew it. And so I did truly behave like a savage out of the forest. For I'll only wed with Medley Plashet.'

Everything in the room shivered away into a silence so intense it might have been a place existing in a dream. This silence seemed to endure an age, an eternity. In the midst of it Medley sat with his writing hand arrested over the paper, and his very mind gasping, fish-like, with anguish and joy and fear.

Then Lewis Mallory, who had been watching his daughter, turned his head slowly towards Medley. He said nothing for a second, but Medley stood up, afraid to look him in the face, but forcing himself to do so.

'And has Medley Plashet spoken to you of this, Catherine?' her father asked very quietly.

'He never would, sir, and that I know. And so I must speak myself, though it damn modesty and niceness,' Catherine said.

Dame Cecily said nothing, but watched her husband.

'We'll write our letter another time, Medley,' Master Lewis said at last. 'Your grandfather asked to see you when you got back. I said I'd send you to him.'

'Now, sir?'

'Now.'

Medley glanced quickly at Catherine, but she was gazing at her locked hands. His glance found Roger. Very faintly, Roger smiled at him. Medley managed to command his feet to carry him out of the room. It seemed to take a long time. At last he had fumbled the door shut behind him. He stood for a second almost reeling, trying to prevent his mouth spreading into a wide, foolish smile. Until a few seconds ago he had been alone with his hopes and despairs for the future, and now Catherine had suddenly moved across to him and stood at his side. It was enough, at the moment, to know this amazing thing had happened. He stood very still, listening—not to what might be said now that he was gone from the room, but to the sound of Catherine's voice echoing inside his own mind—*I'll only wed with Medley Plashet.* She had truly spoken these amazing words. The magnificence of them, their simplicity and truth struck home to him so hard that he had to clap his hands over his mouth as if to prevent his happiness bursting out of him.

Then he acknowledged that the words, however simple, however true, could not have sounded magnificent to Master Lewis or Dame Cecily. And Roger? Medley thanked heaven for two things—that brief smile Roger had given him, and Simon's absence.

Medley roused himself with difficulty, and with his head so far from his feet that he seemed rather to float than walk, he went to see his grandfather.

Judith was outside the cottage, pulling in the washing, just as he remembered his aunt Peg doing all that long time ago, on the day Kit Crespin called at Plashet's, and his mother took him away from the London talk. On that day his whole life had changed its direction.

Judith turned her head as Medley came to the door, looking at him over the linen bundled in her arms. She helped with the washing from the big house, and it struck him as funny in a tender sort of way that there might be some of Catherine's things bundled in with the rest.

'You come back, then?' she said, looking him up and down with a boldness that was new. 'Didn' they want to keep you—once you got right-all-the-way to Lunnon?'

'Keep me? Who?'

'The lords and the ladies. Who else? Did you think I meant the lady Catherine?'

'We brought her home,' he said.

There was something both final and familiar in the words. Medley heard it, and Judith heard it, too. As he watched, the light went out of her face. He might as well have declared himself then and there. Both knew to what he was committed now, for good or ill.

'Your grandfather's been looking out for you,' she said in a low voice. And then she added, lower still, 'So've I, and should know better.'

Because he felt that he had been somehow re-born,

admitted a few steps at least into a world he had never hoped to enter, a world in which he and Catherine existed only for one another, Medley understood and pitied Judith's exclusion. There was nothing he could ever do for her now.

He went indoors to his grandfather, and sat down to tell him something of what he had seen in London—how the broad river ran bright with barges, fast with currents, tumbling into rapids between the straddling legs of the huge bridge. How the houses of the gentry stood along the strand in fair gardens unrolled to the water's edge. He did not speak of the Tower, nor of the Tabard inn, nor of how they had brought Catherine Mallory away from Lord Digby's house. Nor, most certainly, did he speak of what had happened since. But he asked a question.

'When my father first came to Mantlemass to work on the big barn—what was his name?'

Tom Bostel was getting on in years and the question confused him. 'What should it be but what it stayed?' he asked, frowning, a little irritable. 'It's women who should change their name—as he well knew.'

Master Crespin had said *He has yet another name*. That meant, surely, that he had another name than Plashet. Then Medley recalled that his father had had a nickname in his London days—they had called him Richard Plantagenet because of some resemblance to the last king. So perhaps Kit Crespin's remark had merely been the confused rambling of a desperately sick man. Yet he had been positive enough about *the only one left*, and had said his name was Proudless.

Medley left his grandfather and went back to the big house. He went to the little room where he worked with Nicholas Forge. It was empty and quiet, dry as dust, for

everything there was hide and vellum, paper and ink. In
shelves along one wall were the records the secretary had
kept over the years, each year flat between boards and the
boards tied with tape. Here were the household and farm
accounts, the noting of tithes due and paid, the names
of tenants, their marriages, the birth dates of their children, their day of burial. Each messuage was described,
with its dimensions and the service that its tenant owed
the lord of the manor. These in their turn were marked
on a series of maps that stood rolled and tied in a corner.
Medley unrolled the maps one by one and began looking
for Plashet's. Such places soon became known by the
name of their tenant, though on occasion a tenant would
be such a man as men did not easily forget, and then the
property retained the old name. Medley needed to know
what Plashet's had been called before his father went to
it. But though the map of Mantlemass manor had been
re-drawn many times over the years, names altered, new
buildings added, the name on Medley's old home remained Plashet's right back to a map of Dame Elizabeth's
day.

Then at last it seemed clear that his father had taken
a name from the place, not given it his own in the more
customary way.

Medley went to his own small chamber. He pulled out
his father's books and turned the pages vaguely—as if
because his father had handled them they might hold a
secret that could be forced from them. Among them was
the smallest book of all, its pages half empty, the rest
covered with his father's own hand. Could this tell him
anything? He hesitated. He flipped his thumb once
against the pages and then set the little book aside. It was
too private. To look over such pages would surely be like

listening to a man's prayers. Besides, he was half afraid. For what if he read some sentence wrongly, or put his own interpretation on words meant to be differently understood? Every man used words a little in his own way, even though the words themselves could not be changed.

When he had put the books away again, Medley stood staring out of his narrow window. The light was going, but the trees already touched with the beginning of autumn glowed of themselves. A light mist was rising off the forest's marshy places. It was combed in white strands, like unspun flax streaming from the spindle. But further in the valley the mist had folded on itself and become a white sea, out of which the tops of trees rose mysteriously. It was a picture in which nothing was what it seemed. Just so, Medley felt the mists to be drawn over his own existence. He could not know the future, but the past was hidden from him, too.

He heard Roger calling him and found him halfway up the stair to Medley's room.

'Come and speak to my father.'

Medley stared at Roger and his heart turned. 'Has he sent for me?'

'Yes.'

'I must have angered him greatly.'

'Not angered. But troubled. You must never fear him, Medley. He is not a man to fear.'

'Where is—your sister?'

'Tired out and gone to her bed.' Roger smiled. 'I think she startled you more than she startled me.'

'How could I think there'd ever be a time . . . Such words to hear, Roger . . . I must not keep your father waiting.'

'You'll find him in the parlour. Now look up and be

proud, Melly,' Roger said. 'I'd sooner you for my brother than any man in the world.' He gave Medley a hard shove on his way. 'I'll pray for you,' he said, and he grinned; but he meant it.

There was a carved, straight-backed chair by the hearth in the winter parlour. Lewis Mallory was sitting there when Medley came to him. It was unusual to see the lord of Mantlemass sitting in idleness, and Medley knew that he sat so only because he was subdued by the business in hand and troubled in his mind. He realised that Master Lewis must pronounce some judgement, and knew him to be a man who would always turn aside from strictness if he could. No tenant had ever complained of harsh treatment from Lewis Mallory—if any spoke against him it was to call him weak. Nothing could be falser.

Master Lewis sat on in silence a little longer, not even looking up. Then at last he did raise his eyes and straighten his shoulders.

'What am I to say to you?' he asked.

'I have never betrayed your trust in me, sir. Never spoken anything you might not hear.'

'I believe that, Medley. But what shall happen now? You heard what my daughter said.'

'Yes,' said Medley.

'You smile to recall it,' Lewis Mallory said, smiling a little himself. 'Look, boy, I have not forgotten what it is to be young. All the same, this is my only daughter. Shall I marry her to a penniless lad—the grandson of a tenant—the son of a servant of this house? The world is a harsh place, Medley Plashet. There may come a time when the young are let choose their future—but it is not yet. Indeed, it is hard to think how such a state should ever come about—for only the old know how the world goes. Yet for all that,' he said very thoughtfully, 'I myself chose. It was only by the grace of God that I was able to, but I thank heaven for it every hour of my life.' He looked at Medley then, and again a brief smile lifted his sombre expression. 'I have a soft and silly heart, Medley. I wish my children might be happy—as I have been.'

'Sir, I will give all my life to you, and all my service,' Medley said, speaking low and fast. 'I never will go against you or harbour any harsh thought. I shall work and strive only for you and for Mantlemass—fight for you, if need be—if only you will let us stay together. I am young, sir, so, God willing, I have many years of service in me—'

'Oh, Medley,' said Lewis Mallory, laughing a little at this, 'indeed you are very young. Too young yet, I think. Too young to wed.'

'No younger than many, Master Lewis,' said Medley, recalling that this man had himself been married young. 'And not too young to be promised.'

'How long would you wait for her?'

'As long as need be.'

'And she?'

'Would be less kind about that. But she would do it.'

This time Master Lewis gave a kind of chuckle and said he saw that Medley knew the lady well. His manner grew easier and he sat back in his chair. He pulled at a stool with his toe, shoving it towards Medley and ordering him to sit down. 'I am bound to set you a task,' he said. 'Truly your mother was a servant of this house, and her father, too. But your father, Medley, was a strange man from another world. I do not think your name is Plashet, boy, but what it is I cannot say. We never called your father aught but Dick or Richard when he first came here. I think you know well enough that he never saw fit to marry your mother. This, too, I have to remember, though

I do not care to. Family honour is a strange matter. It
cannot be quite ignored . . . Have you any news of your
father? Do you know where he is?'

'Since I was in London I know that he went into
Kent.'

'It disturbs me most that he left you and your mother.
Something from the past made him a fugitive. Find him,
and learn that it was nothing dishonourable. Discover
what your name should have been, had he acknowledged
you. Then return to Mantlemass and tell me what you
know.'

'Shall we be handfast, sir?'

'Not yet.'

'You mean, sir—if there should be some deep dishonour—then I must pay for it?'

'The world goes that way. It is not always my way.
But—yes. I see you understand.' He looked at Medley
gently, with compassion and with liking.

'Yes, sir—I do indeed understand,' Medley answered.
'Unless I can return with honour—then God knoweth it
will be better if I do not return at all.'

11
The Name is Proudless

They had set out so often from Mantlemass, three of them together, that all seemed that morning to be as usual. They would ride for the pleasure of it, or they would be about some errand to the village, or over to Ghylls Hatch. It was only when Medley pulled up on the brow of the high land five or six miles north-east of Mantlemass that the pattern was broken.

'We part here,' he said.

He dismounted and went to stand at Catherine's stirrup. They had not been alone since their return from London. Roger had been their go-between and Roger had stood the brunt of Catherine's anger and anxiety. He had

not wanted her to ride with him and Medley this early
morning, but she had slipped out and caught them up.
She sat now looking down at Medley, still with that pale-
cheeked, glittering-eyed look.

'I'll speak to none till you come back,' she said.

'Pray do,' he said, laughing in spite of everything. 'You
must not lose the habit.'

'Well, return fast, then, that I have no time.'

He did not answer that. It was not so much of a ride
into Kent, if he found what he sought not far over the
border. He could be back in three days, or in three weeks,
or never.

'When you vow, sister,' said Roger, 'choose some
sensible matter.'

'I vow to be true,' said Catherine at once, leaning out
of the saddle towards Medley.

'That's my vow, also,' Medley said. 'And to return with
honour.'

'Anywise you must,' she cried. 'What's your father
to me?'

She gave him her hand, and he took it and held it
briefly, his eyes still searching her face, for even now he
hardly believed the things that had been said. Then he
turned back to his horse and remounted.

'Farewell,' he said.

Catherine and Roger waited side by side as Medley
rode away down the track that dipped into the valley
before rising again to the horizon over which he must
vanish. At the last moment he checked and looked back.
Brother and sister were still waiting there and even at this
distance he could see the steamy cloud from the horses
breathing and snorting in the sharp morning. Medley
raised his arm in a final salute and saw Roger return the
greeting. Catherine did not move. After that, Medley

allowed himself no more dallying, but rode on fast with
a clear image of the two returning side by side to Mantlemass. In his mind, was too, the traitorous fear that he had
possibly trusted his father too lovingly all these years, and
that to find him might be the ruin of his hopes.

A first frost had touched the land and now as the sun
strengthened it caught a thousand spiders' webs, perfect
in pattern, laid over gorse and bracken, and glittering
like silvered embroidery. Medley was riding Cynthus, an
ungrudging loan from Master Orlebar, who would do
anything in this world to please Roger; he had not learnt
yet of his godson's intentions for the future. Medley had
food in his saddlebags and also the book of poems he
knew to be his father's favourite. Last night, Lewis
Mallory had held him firmly by the shoulders and wished
him godspeed and good fortune. So far, all was easy
enough. But soon he would leave the territory he knew
so well and strike out into strange countryside. He was
coming now to the last outpost held by Mantlemass, the
farm called Tillow Holt, kept mostly for sheep rearing,
though they ran a good herd of swine over the forest.
It was at Tillow Holt that Simon had been these last
days, and Medley knew he might see him as he passed.
He would prefer not to see him, for there was far too
much to explain. Yet because Simon lately had begun to
lose his London ways, and seemed to regret his ill temper
towards Medley, it would be a sorry thing to leave,
perhaps for ever, without a word.

Tillow Holt was the end of the true forest, and there
the country opened out into fields and meadows, with
many small farms and steadings. The land was still high.
Looking back at all he knew, Medley saw the forest laid
over that great stretch of undulating country, rich just
now with increasing colour—the bracken dying to a fine

red, the grasses a reedy gold, some beech already moving through yellow to russet, and some cherry already blazing against the quiet dark firs.

Medley had skirted Tillow Holt rather uncertainly, when he saw Simon riding along the boundary. There was a second man riding alongside, and that decided Medley. He slipped into shelter and stayed quiet, watching.

Simon was directing the other rider, with wide sweeps of the arm pointing now this way and now that. It seemed as if the stranger was seeking a way much like the one Medley meant to follow. Watching Simon, Medley saw again how he was slipping back into Mantlemass ways. He looked homespun and farmerly and cheerful—and so Roger had he said would surely be, once the splendours of his stay in London began to be forgotten.

For all this, Medley decided to remain where he was and content himself with watching. Perhaps this second traveller would be a companion for him on the road. Yet he still lingered among the trees, as wary as any forester worth his salt must be. He watched the rider quit Simon and move off. He was a burly man, a little stiff in the saddle, not young, but not old, either. He trotted his horse and looked about him for the way. As he passed the little birch coppice into which Medley had nudged Cynthus, he turned his face full but unseeing in their direction.

At once the whole day, the entire world in which Medley had his present confused being seemed to sharpen and contract. The air hummed with danger. He felt as he had done years ago as he sat listening to Master Crespin talking to his father, and there had suddenly surged over them all a sensation of fear and threat that he had never had the chance to understand.

He did not understand any more now. But he knew

11

that the rider was the man who had called out to Peter
as they left the Tower, 'Is he still alive?' He knew why
the voice had struck that faint and distant and unidenti-
fiable chord in his memory. He could identify it now. It
was the voice of the third stranger, who had held back
to question the boy snivelling in the heather after his
father's rejection.

The pieces of the puzzle began to shift and shuffle as
Medley sat rigid in hiding, his hand on Cynthus's neck
to quiet him lest he whinny to the passing horse. *The
name is Proudless*, Kit Crespin had said, lying on his
wretched bed. And Medley was to tell his father that
there was *only one left*. There seemed to be two possible
reasons for this man to have been waiting at the Tower—
either to get in to Kit Crespin and learn from him where
his half-brother had hidden himself; or to see Dick
Plashet himself arrive and so to make contact with him
once again. Yet the why of all these wherefores remained
utterly obscure to Medley. He could not know why the
only one left sought out Dick Plashet once again, since
he had no knowledge of the reason for his being sought
in the first place. He had nothing but the strange half
explanations his father had given him before he went
away.

Somehow, Medley knew, he must get ahead of the
stranger, and find his father first, and warn him of what
might be coming to him.

As he thought of this, he remembered with alarm his
own likeness to his father. By the encounter outside the
Tower he might have thrown away his father's whole
purpose in denying that he had a son.

The stranger rode on. He was in no hurry, but walked
his horse for long stretches, and paused to look about the
countryside; at the fine view to the south, at a field of

oats not harvested but flattened by some vicious freak of weather, even at a bird singing on a branch as though spring, not autumn, stepped across the land. Behind him, Medley dallied nervously out of sight.

At noon the stranger dismounted, sat under a tree, ate some bread and then lay down to sleep. Medley came up with him faster than he could have wished and almost crashed into the clearing where he lay. At the sight of him, wild ideas possessed Medley—that he would fall upon him and kill him—that he would lead on his horse and leave him to make the best way he could afoot.

The first course was not in his nature, the second too dangerous, for he might have trouble in getting the horse away. He retired, feeling that he lacked boldness, and waited until he saw the man ride away.

At nightfall, the stranger was still ahead, but the suddenly falling dark then swallowed him. Medley rode on alone, nervous and slow, expecting some ambush, aware only now that he did not know where he was going or even how his search should begin. He felt all the loneliness of the novice traveller far from home. He grew sad and sorry for himself, and craven thoughts of giving up came into his mind. But to give up the quest was to give up everything, and that he could never do—unless to redeem his promise to Lewis Mallory and to himself. He would indeed return with honour or not at all. At this thought he found that tears filled his eyes, and he was ashamed of his weakness. He forced himself on, his horse as weary as he was. He came down an incline into a small village, and there ahead of him he saw an inn. He rode into the yard and got stiffly out of the saddle. A servant ran out from the back of the house, calling good evening and

promising supper; and certainly there was a fine smell
of hot food coming from the kitchen. With relief he knew
that the first day was accomplished and the traveller
might rest.

Having learnt from Roger, Medley elected to sleep in
the stable loft. This did not appear to surprise the lad
he had first spoken to, who pulled out fresh straw and
talked to him amiably. His openness was unusual to
Medley, accustomed as he was to the taciturnity of the
foresters. He was glad to talk a little but afraid to talk
too much. After he had eaten his supper at the ordinary,
he called goodnight to the boy and climbed to his bed.
He pulled off his boots and lay down on the straw,
spreading his cloak over him. Below him he heard Cynthus
stamp and blow and that made him feel more comfortable.

This was the first time in his life that Medley had
found himself alone, bound in a nameless direction,
seeking an answer to a question he barely knew how to
express. The loft trap with its swinging hoist was open
to the night sky, and he lay staring out, now at the stars,
now down into the yard and across to the inn building,
where lights still showed and voices were raised. No other
traveller came in darkness to the inn, only as the sky
began to lighten and Medley lay still awake, a man led
a lame horse in and shouted for attention. Even in that
dim light, Medley saw who had come.

'Food and a bed,' the man demanded of the lad who
came tousled and yawning in answer to his cry. 'See to
the horse. I'll need a smith come morning.'

'Go indoors, sir,' the boy said, leading the horse to
the stable.

The lad came into the stable just below Medley, who
slid through his straw to the inner trap and gazed down

the ladder. The boy had hung a lantern by the head of the
stall next to Cynthus, and now he began to rub down
the horse, soothing and whistling as he did so.

'Swollen fetlock,' Medley said from above his head.

The boy grinned up at him. 'I'd forgot you. Not much
swole. Loose shoe, no other matter. It's a good animal,
carelessly rid. Not like your fine fellow.'

'The rider,' said Medley, his heart in his mouth. 'Was
that Master Proudless?'

'I never saw him till now. Only Proudless I know lives
nearly to Ashford. Would they be kin?'

Medley frowned. Master Crespin had said so firmly
only one. He had not bargained for more. Then he
wondered if this traveller in fact was some quite other
man, nothing to do with the business at all, whose face
he had seemed to know because he was nervous and ripe
to see danger everywhere.

'What other Proudless is it you know?' he asked.

'A man much in demand. He's about the countryside
all the time—here and there and everywheres. There's
many great houses building at this time. Proudless can
turn his hand to any building skill—masonry, carpentry—
even pargeting and thatching. He's a rare fellow, indeed.
Is he the one you're seeking?'

'Yes,' said Medley. 'I think it may be.' The blood was
pumping in his temples now and he had broken into a
sweat that made him shiver. He heard again Kit Crespin's
sick and weary voice telling him *The name is Proudless*.
He had simply mistaken the application. It was not his
enemy who was so called. It was his father.

Medley slept no more, but lay waiting for the light to
increase. At the first possible moment he rose, saddled
up Cynthus and led him out. There was no stirring yet

from the inn, but he had made his reckoning overnight
and found no difficulty in setting out with an empty
stomach. The morning was cold and overcast, the wind
had changed and promised rain. He was still shivering
after he had ridden a mile and more down the road,
excitement adding to the chill of the weather and his
fasting condition. He needed to find the name Ashford
on a milepost, and found none with any name at all. He
rode on knowing only that his general direction was
right. The morning was fully come before he reached a
village where he could ask the way, and found himself
many miles from his objective. However, the stable lad
had said *nearly* to Ashford, not beyond. So he would
ask at every village he came to, whether one Proudless
lived thereabouts. As he rode, he was conscious that
another would soon be on the road, that he might know
the way better, even if he was not sure where it was
to end.

Rain set in about noon, and the hours from then till
dusk were increasingly uncomfortable. It seemed to
Medley that he had travelled too far north, and wasted
his time. In the villages he passed, no one seemed able
or willing to help him. As darkness fell, however, he
came to a village with a friendly face. A church stood on
a mound, a green before it, a biggish farm bordering that,
a few cottages, a forge. It was at the forge he asked for
Proudless, speaking the name now with a feeling of
unreality, for who could say that the name might not be
his own.

'The whole world asks for'm,' the smith said.

'Who else—today?'

'A biggish gentleman brought his horse in—some time
after noon. Trouble with a shoe yesterd'y, so he said—and
so I should think! I told him he should not ride the beast

yet awhile. I poulticed the leg and he walked off to the inn.'

'He'll not find Proudless there,' said Medley boldly. 'Will he?'

'Is it Proudless the mason?'

'Yes. That Proudless.'

'No, then he'll not find him there. You want another ten mile to where Proudless lives—if he's at home, for he finds himself much in demand—a skilled man, sir, and worth any gentleman's waiting for—should he be thinking to build him a fine house. As many do, for there's wealth abroad these days. New gentry in the making.'

Medley thanked him for his help and rode on. The rain had ceased. The night was warm and scented with the end of the year. He must have come many miles out of his way that his fellow traveller, with a lame horse, had arrived at the same spot ahead of him. But now he was mewed up for the night. Medley rode Cynthus hard until the last light went, then looked for a bed. He knew now that the stranger riding his way had information more than his. He knew, almost certainly, that it was Proudless he, too, sought. He was the *only one left*, and his purpose seemed hatefully clear. So Medley put as much distance between them as he could.

That was an uncomfortable night, fleas in the straw, a pie of bones and gristle for supper, and long sleepless hours to follow. But in those hours the sky cleared altogether. The cold increased, and in the bright morning that followed, frost was on every blade of yellowing grass. Medley and Cynthus rode out rejoicing. Three miles down the road, the sun well up and warming his back, he asked a woman in a cottage garden if she knew anything of Proudless.

'Dick Proudless,' she said. 'You'll find where he lives

two mile more up the road.' She smiled and nodded, as if it gave her pleasure to help him. 'A fine man,' she said, and his heart swelled.

He thanked her and rode on, east out of the village on a road that dwindled until it almost disappeared, running then, the width of a cart, through an expanse of hazel and birch wood. The woods closed behind him as the track turned, and then he saw ahead in a clearing a small cottage, not much more than a hovel, but with a chimney set against the wall which suggested a skilful builder had been at work. There was smoke rising from the chimney, and as Medley rode slowly, almost timidly forward, a man came from the open door, yoked up two buckets and went to the nearby well.

Medley checked Cynthus and stood for a second. He had not seen his father for several years, and they had been years of great change for both of them. Sometimes he had wondered if he recalled Dick Plashet clearly any longer, and he feared he might be uncertain when they met. But the instant he saw him, his back turned, walking away in the opposite direction, his hair rather whiter, his figure a little thicker than memory had shown it, Medley's doubts were done.

He nudged Cynthus forward quietly. His father was busy with the buckets and heard nothing. He paused when the first bucket was up and looked above his head into the branches. Here there was a tree well grown and a squirrel was in the branches, stripping off a nut. Most men would have aimed a stone at the creature, for there was a kind of war waged daily by men against natural things that Medley had learnt from his mother to hate. Dick Plashet—Dick Proudless—however he wanted to be called, held his hand as Anis or Medley would have done, and Medley thought he was laughing.

He dismounted and tethered his horse. He took the book of Latin poems from his saddlebag and slid it into the pouch at his belt. Then he walked towards the well.

This time the leaves rustled under his feet and his father turned. He stood quite still, gazing at Medley, looking him over slowly, head to toe. However little he himself might have changed, his son had grown almost to a different being. The older man was the uncertain one now.

He frowned slightly, took a step forward and then paused. 'Medley?'

'Yes, father,' Medley said. Tears came into his eyes and he ran forward. His father stood still with his hands at his sides. Medley clasped him and kissed him. Then he stood back at arms' length, gripping his father by the shoulders. 'Look!' he cried. 'I'm taller than you now. I can give you a head and more!'

His father did not reply. His face was expressionless, his eyes cold.

'I have offended you, sir,' Medley said, his confidence leaving him.

'I gave up all I had won so that you might forget I had ever existed.' He stammered very slightly, a fault that Medley had forgotten could appear in his speech when he was moved. 'I denied my whole self to give you a life of your own.'

'I should not have expected you might be glad to see me.'

'Indeed you should not. It is not as my son you must live—I told you that long ago.'

'But you did say I am your son. However you want to be quit of me—you said I could be sure of that.'

'I still say so.' He looked deeply at Medley and frowned. 'Take a mirror, boy, and see how little use there'd be in denying that! But there's no virtue in it for you.'

'I'm grown now,' Medley cried, 'and I need to know
many things.' He grew bolder as he spoke, almost hating
his father for the rebuff he had given. Anger drove out
disappointment and he felt strong. 'There's my life to
live now in the way I've chosen. I am no longer a child,
sir, and childish answers are not for me now.'

A faint smile flicked over his father's face, the first hint
of human warmth. 'You have made some way in the world,
I see. Where's your country talk now?'

'Back of my mind,' said Medley.

'What does your mother think of you?'

'My mother died.'

'Ah, my poor Anis—my poor Anis,' Dick said in a
low voice. 'I might as well have killed her with my own
hand. She had most to bear. I never should have stayed
with any woman, or seen any child to call my own. God
rest her. I loved her dear.' He turned away and went
towards the cottage as if he needed to be alone. But at
the door he paused and beckoned Medley in.

All was neat in that modest place. As at Plashet's there
was a window made up of glass carefully collected. The
hearth was tidy, the fire quietly burning, peat and wood
stacked in the ingle. There was a small scrubbed table, a
bed built against the wall, two stools, a couple of cooking
pots. The place was meagre without being mean—a place
in which a man of pride lived without a woman to care
for him.

Medley held out the book he had brought with him.

'I saved them all,' he said. 'You will have been needing
this one a long time.'

His father took the book and opened it instantly, turning the pages almost tenderly. 'You recalled this was my
favourite? And you—have you remembered your lessons?'

'I can read as well as you, I daresay, sir. Master Mallory

took me to Mantlemass when my mother died. I work with old Nicholas Forge. In time, I may have his place. If all goes well,' he added.

'I could not have chosen better for you.'

'Your choice was to desert me,' Medley countered.

'Well—you have found me. What do you expect of me?'

'That you'll tell me my name—Plashet or Proudless or whatever in this world it may be.'

'And besides?'

'I must know if you fled for the sake of honour or because of dishonour. I have not forgotten all you told me once—that there was nothing I might safely inherit from my own father. *Safely* is the word I most remember. You must see it is all a mystery to me. Three strangers came for you, but you escaped them. You denied I was your son, then told me that this at least was truth. The strangers came again—and you fled . . . I cannot know what to make of all this, sir . . . I have a message for you. From—from your brother.'

'Have I a brother?'

'Your half-brother.'

'Kit? Kit Crespin?'

'I am to tell you *There is only one left.*'

'Where did you see Kit?'

'I saw him in the Tower of London, father; very near to death. They would not kill him, he said, but they would let him die. He told me of your kinship.'

'What else?'

'Only the message.' Medley gave his father a sharp, cold look. 'He greeted me more kindly than you have done.'

'Only one left. But which? Which?'

'A man more square than round, short and strong. His hair the colour of iron. Not young.'

'Then you have seen him.'

'I believe I have. Father—why was Master Crespin in the Tower?'

'For the same reason that I might have been there myself. But they would have killed me. For the safety of the state . . . Poor Kit—he would never skulk as I have done. Things went well for him, but they were bound to change. We have a new King now—and he has no son . . . This *only one*, Medley—where have you seen him?'

'At the Tower, when he called out to the landlord's son who took me. "Is he still alive?" he called . . . Then on the way here—'

'He has followed you!'

'He was ahead. Then his horse went lame. He was delayed. I am certain he never saw me.'

'He has seen Kit and now he knows where I am. He will find his way here, for sure.'

Medley watched his father walk restlessly about the room, pausing at last to gaze out of the open door at the quiet woodland. It was as if he had decided there was not much time and that he must speak before the next link in the chain was forged. Medley felt his own muscles tightening, his mind holding itself in readiness for what it must learn. He grew very frightened, his heart beating so hard that it muffled his hearing, and he was glad of it, as if he need not hear what might be the ending of his hopes. Years ago, on the day they had spoken together so deeply and bitterly, his father had disclaimed any fault. But that was before he went away, seeming to run from danger. *What I have done for you*, he had said then, when Medley cried out against his bastardy, *is better a thousand times than what the world might do* . . . He had believed in his father ever since, though at times with difficulty. His whole life and happiness depended on what his father might tell him now of the past, and so for the first time his doubts came clear into the open, magnified by fear a hundred times. He almost sprang up and burst from the place, to mount and ride away in ignorance—for that seemed better by far than what he might be going to learn.

Now his father had begun to speak and escape was cut off. His voice was very low and monotonous, the words wrung out of him like a confession extracted under torture. He spoke of his childhood, of believing himself the son of country folk—of being fetched away without an hour's warning and taken to the house of a Dr Woodlark.

'I was there six years, learning all the time about everything but myself. Then it was late summer—the harvest month. A man came to the door bringing a horse for me to ride. I had never seen him before, though I had seen others concerned with my well-being. "My friends call me Kit," he said. It was not for years I knew he was my brother.'

The low, almost sad voice continued then with more animation, telling how they two had ridden out through the late evening, and through the night, till they came to a place where an army was encamped, and all about was the sound of preparation for a battle. A hundred and more fine tents stood up in the early dawn, while all the countryside waited for what was to come.

'Kit told me I should see my father. He took me through the press of lords and captains to a far tent. We were allowed to enter. There was a table spread with maps, and three or four gentlemen studying the maps, bending over the table, pointing now here, now there. They were half armed. I remember a page standing polishing a helmet, and how he stared at me. Then someone said, "This is the boy, sir." And one of them turned. He was sturdy and dark and I knew him, for his face was mine—as yours is mine—and his. "I'll talk to him alone," he said. And all the rest withdrew.'

Medley watched his father turn from the open door and lean against the jamb as if he needed support. His face was white and his eyes shone with recollection. He seemed to force himself to continue his story.

'He s-said, "Tomorrow may be my last battle. If I live, I promise to acknowledge you as my son. But if I die—then go at once and hide yourself, for some will seek to kill you, while others will want you for their tool." Then,' said Dick Plashet, 'I looked and saw the device he wore upon his surcoat, and I saw the great ring on his finger, and his helmet lying by. And near it something so magnificent I remember crying out at the sight of it, "Is it true? Is it true?" It was the crown—the royal crown of England lying there—that he was to wear into battle. The battle was fought on Bosworth Field. My father was the King—and my name, like his, was Richard Plantagenet.'

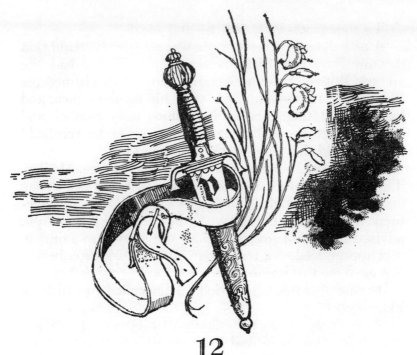

12
Ending With Medley

Medley sat in silence, shivering, his hands gripped together, saying over and over in his mind, 'I am King
Richard's grandson. I am a Plantagenet. I am royal and
might have been called Prince, even though I was born
out of wedlock.' Then Kit Crespin's riddle fell into place.
He, Medley, was *the sprig of broom*, a branch of *planta
genista*, whose flower was the Plantagenet emblem.

The silence grew and stretched between him and his
father. It seemed an age in time before Medley managed
to ask,' Why was I not to know ?Why could you not tell
me the truth?'

'Where there is a throne there is always dispute.'

'To touch us—you, father—and me?'

'A new dynasty, a new house was set over England that day on Bosworth Field, when Henry Tudor had the victory. But you know well enough how many claimed the Plantagenet right—and made their bid for the crown, and lost it—and their heads. Far more than Simnel and Warbeck—others whose names may never be recalled.'

'But could this have touched you and me?'

'Those three strangers were no strangers to me, Medley. They were kin of my mother and they saw me as a strong claimant to the English throne. It was their own advancement they sought, not mine . . . But I did as Kit Crespin advised me. I hid myself among the crowds in London, was apprenticed to a tradesman. I was Dick Proudless— Kit gave me that name. But I was too like my father.'

'I remember!' Medley cried. 'They called you Richard Plantagenet.'

'Aye—in sport, as they thought, nicknaming a fellow apprentice. I grew afraid then, afraid of myself—and I ran even from Kit. When the chance came, when some of my skills were sought to build in the countryside—then I came to the forest—to Mantlemass. England became the country of the Tudors. The Plantagenets were almost forgotten.'

'You were safe there . . . Until the day Master Crespin found you—?'

'He came to warn me. I'd lived in a fool's paradise supposing my kinsmen had no notion where I was. They let me alone only because the time was not ripe. But that summer, Medley, young De la Pole, who was nephew to King Edward IV, was sent to the Tower. And there to this day he still lies. So it was that year my kinsmen sought me out because then there was no better claimant. I had only one care—believe this, Medley—I feared greatly that if they knew I had a son they might take him for their man in my stead.'

'To make him King of England?' Medley said slowly.

'To attempt it.'

'To make *me* King of England, father?'

'I saw the likeness growing. Thank God that day you were questioned you looked dirty and ruffianly—and the daylight was almost gone.'

Medley laughed out loud, it all sounded so wildly fanciful. Yet he knew well that young Simnel had been a lad of little importance when he was set up with his court in exile by those who sought the downfall of the Tudors. At least he had escaped with his life, even if not with his pride. The rest had lost their heads . . . Involuntarily, Medley's hand went to his throat and he wondered how it was when your head was struck from your body as you knelt at the block. He looked at his father with fondness yet with great puzzlement.

'I never could have heeded them,' he said. 'Any more than you.'

'Now I see you grown I can believe that,' his father said slowly. 'You are stronger than I. Indeed—I do see that most clearly.'

'How—stronger?'

'I was tempted,' said his father harshly. 'I ran from my weakness to save my head. I was tempted—tempted. I saw the grandeur of it all far more than I saw the folly. For years, until you were a grown lad, my life was a fight with my own ambition. Then, thank God, it became a fight to save you from yours.'

'From my ambition?' Medley shook his head. 'How could I be ambitious when I knew nothing?' He spoke gently, for this revelation of weakness in a man he had thought so strong moved him greatly, both to pity and

to a new love. 'I am a forester, father. I could never be
anything else. Truly, I am no longer a hind, as I might
have been—but I never want more than to live where I
was born. How could I be tempted by something I could
never one quarter understand?'

'Ah, but you have not heard these men—these per-
suaders—the glittering pictures they draw so well . . .'

'Perhaps,' said Medley, 'it was my mother taught me
to trust myself. For I do.'

Now for a score of reasons he began to feel a great
lifting of the spirit. Because there was no dishonour—
because he was sure of himself as, most strangely, he saw
now that his father had never been; because he had a tale
to tell that seemed to offer more than it took away. Only
the sadness of Anis's suffering remained, and she perhaps
had loved too well to care greatly about her chance of
heaven. Yet they had both, mother and son, been the
victims not of his father's strength but of his weakness
and self-doubt. Medley swallowed the surge of bitterness
that threatened for a moment to overcome his prouder
feelings as he thought of his mother. Then he came to
consider how strange it would have been to her to know
certainly that her son shared blood with the Lion-heart,
with Edward, whom men had named the Black Prince;
and most strangely of all, he realised as he fumbled with
the memory of old tales told in his schooldays, with that
Plantagenet John of Gaunt, Duke of Lancaster, who had
been lord over all the forest before York and Lancaster
stirred into drawn-out warfare. It might almost be said
that in Medley, as in the present King Henry, York and
Lancaster were made one. Truly his blood was more
nearly shared with that King Richard who had been called
a monster and a murderer, but for sure it was with John
of Gaunt, who had hunted and ridden the same forest

tracks as those Medley knew, that he must forever feel the keenest affinity . . .

His father was saying quietly, as if he read his thoughts, 'Whatever else, King Richard was a man of courage. He fought that day like ten men, but ten was not enough. I saw them take his body from the field—thrown over a horse's back, gashed and almost naked . . .' He pulled from his belt the neat small dagger he had worn there every day that Medley could recall, and he laid it on the table. 'He gave me this. He had a way of pulling it half from its sheath as he talked, and slipping it back again—so Kit Crespin told me. But that cold early morning—for it was cold with fear—he unbuckled it and gave it to me. You will see it has *P* for Plantagenet, with a crown above.'

'P stood for Proudless, too. And for Plashet.'

'I had to be rid of Proudless when I went first into hiding. Plashet was the name of the holding Master Mallory gave me and Anis. It was near enough to make me feel often that it was indeed Plantagenet, but mangled by the local tongue.'

'So I shall always think,' said Medley softly. 'But my children shall be called Medley, and the rest forgotten.' Without pausing to think what he was doing, he went on his knees and took his father's hand and kissed it, and set his own forehead against it, as if in fealty. 'I shall pray to do as well by my son as you have done by yours,' he said.

'Well, God bless you, and whoever comes after,' his father said quietly. 'I would your mother were here. She never knew why I denied her her dearest right.' He drew Medley to his feet and kissed him. 'It is best not to meet again,' he said.

'It is only now we know each other!' Medley cried.

'It is best. There is still my kinsman—*the only one left*. Besides, I have made my life here, and here I shall stay.

Go back to the forest and live as you have chosen, in your turn.' He was silent a moment. 'And I shall not see Kit Crespin again, alas.'

'His life was easier than yours, sir. Yet he, too, could call himself Plantagenet.'

'He had no sponsors, and was the happier for it. His mother was a serving wench with a pretty face. Mine was gently born, poor soul. Her kinsmen claim that Richard Plantagenet wed her secretly and that he wed his Queen in sin. Who can tell? He told me so, truly—but he needed a son by then and men will say anything in extremity.' He gave Medley a smile both sad and tender. 'Get on your way. For your happiness and mine, forget your blood as you have promised. They say the present King will never sire a son—foolish talk, maybe, but talk to spark new ambitions. *The only one left* knew what he was doing, Medley, when he came out of London on your heels.'

Then he stopped short and looked up sharply. He moved quietly to the door and stood there gazing out cautiously into the woodland. 'A horseman passed on the far side of the quarry,' he said very softly. 'Now he has turned from the track that could have carried him northward, out of our way. He is returning by the lower path . . . For sure, Medley, *the only one left* is already here.'

The big man with his iron-grey hair stood on the doorstep, and he and Richard smiled at one another without friendliness.

'Well, cousin,' Richard said. 'A surprise, though not a pleasant one. Have you business in these parts?'

'Possibly I have business in these parts . . . You've aged, cousin. Though not so sorely and finally as poor Kit Crespin.'

'Ah, poor Kit . . . I was assured you must have spoken
with poor Kit.'

'I was ever one for getting doors unlocked, cousin
Richard. You know that. Dying men ramble. Proudless,
he said, poor fellow—taking me to be I know not who.
And Kent. And Medley, he said. And Mantlemass. And
Anis dead . . . Such items make a map for a man accustomed to find his way.' Then he looked past Richard to
Medley standing a little back and behind his father. 'You
could not fool me now as you fooled me once,' he said.
'Good God in heaven, the boy's his grandfather to the
life. All but something about the mouth—a softness. He
has that, no doubt, from his mother.'

'Not my wife, the world would say, cousin.'

'And not the first man born out of wedlock and bound
for high places.'

As he spoke, he shouldered indoors and stood looking
Medley up and down. 'The instant I heard they had Kit
Crespin in the Tower, I knew I had only to wait. I
expected you to come visiting, Richard. I got more than
I bargained for.'

He began to walk round Medley, eyeing him up and
down with an expression sharp and bounding with confidence. Medley stirred and scowled.

'Have you seen all you want now, sir?'

'Look at him, cousin Richard! Look at him! When I
saw him by the Tower I could hardly believe my good
fortune. But look at him, I say! Twice as good a likeness
as you can offer. Build—well, taller and straighter, but
still the weight's much the same, or will be soon. Colouring, too. And the way he lowers his head a little to look
beneath his brows . . . He smiles too much—his laugh, I
daresay, is too merry. But any man would know him.
There are Yorkists by the thousand still from south to

north and across from side to side of England—and every one would rise and follow the instant they set eyes on him.'

'Bless us,' mocked Richard, 'is this how you come again to offer me the throne?'

'Not you, cousin. There's no need of you now. I'll take the youngster.'

'Where, sir?' asked Medley, very cool.

'To the throne of England, boy! To wear a crown! To order and command men! To wed a princess of the blood royal and get sons to carry the name of Plantagenet firm into the future.'

Medley laughed. 'I shall not say "Get thee behind me".'

'Ah—then you have twice your father's spirit—who was tempted, but a coward.'

'I shall not say it because I have no need.'

'We'll raise the standard in the north. There's most support there and they'll come riding like madmen. Have you ever commanded men? Ever worn fine silk? Ever snapped your fingers for what you fancy? You shall do it soon.'

'Keep your crown—cousin, am I to call you?'

'You've bred him to be modest, cousin Richard.'

'Keep your crown,' Medley said again, and now his voice rose. 'Keep your throne of England and I'll keep my own life and live it the way I choose. There's no treasure you can offer me, surelye—a countryman, sir, a forester with treasures of his own.' As he spoke, his father standing quite silent, Medley's boldness grew in him, and he thought that so he might have spoken if his grandfather had not died on Bosworth Field, if his father had inherited and he in turn had been his father's heir. He seemed to feel himself grow taller and broader, harsher and more commanding. His chin lifted and his eyes hardened and the last boyishness went out of him because he knew he was facing an enemy. 'Get you away from here,' he said between his teeth, 'and see you never come again—not to my father—not to me. For we have neither any need of you.' He saw the little dagger with P for Plantagenet below the incised crown, lying where his father had laid it on the table. He stretched out his hand and picked it up, unsheathed, and it fitted so snugly to his palm and fingers that it could have been forged and fashioned just for him. 'Now this shall be mine,' he said. 'Keep far from it, cousin traitor. I've slit the throat of a hart-royal before now. I know where to strike and how to keep a blade keen till it's needed.'

The big man laughed, it sounded so grand, but the laugh was not easy. He stood abruptly still, flicking his glance from son to father, a man suddenly aware of being on his own, a conspirator whose cause had dwindled, not all at once, perhaps, but unadmittedly, and whose support had gone, had vanished into a dream world fed only by vanity. A few years ago he could indeed have ridden the country-side summoning thousands to the old banner—he could have done that and so he would have sworn readily. Yet now he looked as solitary standing there as the old stags Medley had seen driven out by younger rivals, shifting away with the fight gone out of them, their eyes blearing and their bones already chilled.

'Keep your toy dagger,' he said at last, 'and deny your blood if you must. Then we can call each other traitor and cry quits.'

'Go now, cousin,' Richard said, breaking his silence, but quite gently. 'Go now.'

The man struggled with his pride, with the sad defeat of time that had taken away his strength. 'You shall not have a second chance,' he cried to Medley, as if this threat was a final but certain weapon. 'If I go now, I never come again. There'll be no second chance, I tell you, young Plantagenet.'

'A bastard Plantagenet, master,' Medley said, slipping into his forester's tongue. 'Not the first, maybe, come you said, sir, but a countrified kind. A fine grummut of a king they'd reckon me, surelye. A solly sort of prince. Not a dezzick worth the doing, master, that's for sure.'

The *only one left* opened his mouth as if to shout an answer, but he closed it again. He flung towards the door, and again hesitation overtook him, and he tripped at the threshold. Surprisingly, his cousin caught him by the elbow and checked his fall.

'Farewell, then, kinsman,' he said.

'Farewell,' the other muttered, 'Richard Plantagenet.'

He was gone then, and the two stood watching and listening as he went back to his horse, and mounted clumsily, and rode away, the horse stumbling once, as if he took his mood from his rider.

'Now you go, too,' his father said to Medley. 'Go home where you belong. Tell the tale once, if you must. Then let it be forgotten.'

'And shall you never tell it again, sir?' Medley asked.

'I'll need to be an old, old man before vanity drags it from me.' He turned away and picked up the worn book of poems that Medley had returned to him. His thumb flicked again tenderly at the pages he could hardly wait to read. 'Get home to Mantlemass,' he said.

When Cynthus breasted the high ground by Tillow Holt the forest was spread ahead of him and his rider. It was early morning, for they had been on the moonlit road all night. Now that moon still hung in a sky so soft and full that it seemed to billow out of the heavens like a vast

curtain. Stars had long vanished. The September sun
rose up behind Medley as he rode and gave the moon its
final, borrowed brilliance. It was a sun half red, half gold,
and the light it shed revived the fallen bracken, red and
wet, so that the forest seemed spread with fire. The trees
leapt in their early autumn beauty, and across the great
arc of the sky, five swans flew bright as mercury towards
the waters of the pond over to the north-west.

Medley pulled Cynthus to a halt and looked about him.
This was his world, not London or those places where
men plotted for power, nor the country his father had
chosen; not even the far downs where the sea was held
in check. The forest opened up for him with a power that
would warm but never consume him. It was far from the
strangeness and the grandeur and the fear of a few hours
ago, and his face slit into a smile, his heart lightened. He
looked to the far slopes of this familiar country, for there
lay all his hope and all his future.

He twitched the rein and began quite slowly to descend
the long track from the upland to ride beside the river,
and then to cross it at the ford, and then again to mount
the winding hollow way towards Mantlemass. Already
there was a stirring about the forest, for the sun, so
reluctant in its first yawn over the horizon, had then
rushed up into the blue, the pink light had vanished and
only a fine clear day was left of the dawn's enchantment.

Riding this way, Medley went past Master Urry's great
iron-working. He saw Hal walking down towards the
hammer, and Hal spotted him and waved and shouted.
Medley waved back, but found he could not shout, and
maybe Hal looked a little dashed. It must seem to him
that his old schoolfellow had grown a trifle grand and
staid, riding a borrowed horse, but a fine one, in a good
dark doublet and soft boots . . .

He came up to the manor by way of the old coney warrens that stretched both sides of this small river which he and Roger had so often fished. There was a fisherman there now. It was Simon, wearing an old red cap of his father's. He looked very far from the insolent London gallant of the early summer. He turned at the sound of the horse. At once, seeing his face open and unguarded, Medley knew that things had changed in some way for him, too.

Medley checked Cynthus, and Simon set his line to look after itself and came slowly up the bank. A strange sensation of power moved in Medley then. He imagined himself indeed a prince and Simon his subject, who should pull off his cap as he approached and perhaps go down humbly on one knee. The prince would raise his subject with a generous gesture of one ringed hand, and hold out that hand for his subject to kiss in expression of loyalty and allegiance. So it had been with generations of his blood, thought Medley, a little light-headed with the power of his imagination, and so it might have been with him, had fate so moved . . .

Simon came up and laid his hand on Cynthus's bridle, looking up at Medley and certainly never thinking to bare his head.

'I wondered if we should see you again,' he said.

'And rejoiced that you might not?'

'No,' said Simon. He frowned a little, as if disturbed by the challenge. His face remained, however, friendly and familiar, the face Medley had known for years before life in London wrought its changes in Master Mallory's elder son. There was still the touch of arrogance, but the very slightness of it was a blessing after what had gone before. 'Did you know Roger would leave us, Medley?'

'I knew his purpose . . .' A sad cold touch was about Medley's heart then. 'So he has gone.'

'The day after you went away he told his purpose. He left at once, long, long before my mother could dry her tears. As if he planned it for the time he would be most missed.'

'More one time than another?' Medley cried, and heard himself groan for the loss of his dearest friend.

'Medley,' said Simon, twice his old self now, 'I know that I have treated you sore. Perhaps I felt Roger was more your brother than mine . . . But he has taught me much that I had forgotten. It costs me nothing, I find, to tell you I am glad you have come home.'

Medley dismounted, for it seemed necessary that they should stand level and eye one another as equals.

'Is this indeed my home?' he asked. 'And shall you always feel so kindly?'

'I shall hope to. Though mostly,' said Simon with a faint grin, 'men quarrel from time to time. And so shall we, for sure.' Then he looked Medley very straight in the eye and said honestly and openly, 'My father is short of a son now. My mother needs comfort, though the loss is so sanctified. They will welcome you. I know it. And my sister—well, that you know already . . . Tell me, was your search fruitful—did you find your father?'

'I found him.' He might have said: And I found myself. He stood steady with Simon, and he hugged his royal blood vein by vein. 'I have nothing to tell of him that need shame the Mallorys, Simon. But I am still a bastard and still a penniless suitor.'

'How much of his purpose did Roger tell you?'

'Why—that he would go into the church—that he would go to the Benedictines at St Pancras . . .'

'Men give up all their possessions when they enter such

a life—as well you know. Did Roger never tell you who should be his heir?'

'He told me nothing more.'

'It is you, Medley. He has named you.'

Medley was stunned into silence, the blood, royal or common, draining out of his cheeks as if he faced some dreadful peril instead of news so extraordinary.

'You know that Master Orlebar gave Ghylls Hatch to my father in trust for Roger. So now Roger hands the trust to you.'

'Ghylls Hatch,' muttered Medley. Instinctively he laid his hand along Cynthus's fine strong neck.

'Master Orlebar loves Roger so well he would do anything in this world to please him. He is very willing that you should be his heir. He must have known, he says, when he gave you your riding-boots . . . And my father is happy in the arrangement, too,' Simon said, for Medley seemed unable to say a word. 'So there has been great anxiety for your return. The only fear was that there might be some dishonour that had caused your father's flight.' He took Medley's arm and shook him. 'Wake up. You are no longer a penniless suitor!'

'Truly I am no longer a pauper,' Medley said faintly. 'Will you forget, then, that I am not in law the son of any man?'

'God's truth, there have been many such, and in the highest places. I'll take my brother's value of you, Medley Plashet. Remember the old days, when even I was at school, and we played York and Lancaster? You were York, and you were small and weak—but sometimes you still found ways to win. Which was against history . . . Well—so it is now.'

Medley hesitated. The words rushed to his tongue— but stayed there. I am Medley Plantagenet. My father is

Richard Plantagenet, claimed as the lawful son of King Richard . . . The little bright dagger was hanging at his belt; he put his hand to it, and shifted it in its sheath as Kit Crespin had described his grandfather shifting it, in and out, in and out as he talked. He was glad he had it— with the *P* and the crown, to show his good master, Lewis Mallory, and then perhaps to hide away for ever, as he would hide his knowledge of his blood.

'Will you get up to Mantlemass now?' Simon said. 'And see you dry my sister's tears. One way and another we've had a tedious, wailing time of it since you went away.' He frowned at Medley, the sun in his eyes. 'You have my blessing,' he said, with a last flourish of fine manners.

'I thank you for it,' said Medley, bowing slightly. He glanced down the bank at the fishing-line. 'Have you had good sport, brother?'

'No, brother. A little perch two fingers thick. I threw it back to grow for your wedding breakfast.'

He turned his back at that; as he went off down to the water Medley saw that he was laughing.

Medley rode on his way. His head was full of glories. Trumpets sounded in his ears and bright banners curled and flapped in the fine keen wind of his imagination.

Note

A Certain Richard Plantagenet . . .

Between the years 1544 and 1546 Sir Thomas Moyle was building himself a great house at Eastwell in Kent. He had been Speaker of the House of Commons in the reign of Henry VIII and held various other statesmanly offices in the following reigns. He had amassed a fortune by the middle years of the century and was consolidating his position as a country gentleman and landowner. Like any other gentleman in his situation, he liked to visit the site and see how things were going, to discuss matters with the builders and so on. At these times he noticed that one of the builders, a man of sixty or so, would settle down apart from the rest while they gossiped over their bread and cheese, and spend the break in working hours reading—reading, moreover, in a book of Latin verse.

Sir Thomas became increasingly interested, intensely curious, and at last he questioned the man, asking his name and story. After some hesitation, the man told Sir Thomas the tale that Medley heard from his father. For this was Richard Plantagenet in his declining years, still working, still solitary. Sir Thomas was greatly moved by the tale and urged Richard to make himself free of the hospitality of the splendid new Eastwell Place. However, a lonely life had left Richard disinclined for much company. He asked instead that he might build himself a small dwelling-place within the grounds. This request was gladly granted, and Richard spent his remaining years at Eastwell. He died when he was 'upwards of Fourscore'.

Anno Domini 1550, runs the entry in the Parish Register of Eastwell. *Rychard Plantagenet was buried the twenty-second Day of December Anno ut Supra.*

Eastwell Church, in the grounds of the big house, has fallen into ruin. Precisely where Richard was buried we shall probably never discover, though tradition marks the spot and some years ago a bush of broom was planted there, and a white rose for York. What became of him between the Battle of Bosworth in 1485 and his encounter with Sir Thomas Moyle in the 1540s is equally open to conjecture. This story of *The Sprig of Broom* imagines what might have happened in the unrecorded middle years of his life.